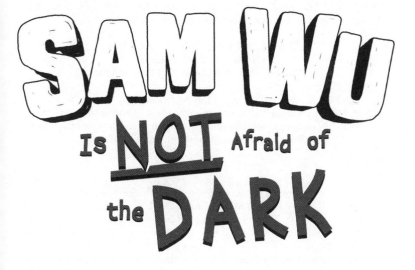

STERLING CHILDREN'S BOOKS
New York

An Imprint of Sterling Publishing Co., Inc.
1166 Avenue of the Americas
New York, NY 10036

ISBN 978-1-4549-3371-7

Distributed in Canada by Sterling Publishing co., Inc.
c/o Canadian Manda Group, 664 Annette Street
Toronto, Ontario, M6S 2C8, Canada

For information about custom editions, special sales, and premium and
corporate purchases, please contact Sterling Special Sales at 800-805-5489
or specialsales@sterlingpublishing.com.

Manufactured in China
Lot #:
2 4 6 8 10 9 7 5 3 1
05/19

sterlingpublishing.com

SAM WU

IS NOT Afraid of the DARK

I am totally OKAY!!! with this!

KATIE & KEVIN TSANG
Illustrated by Nathan Reed

STERLING CHILDREN'S BOOKS
New York

FOR OUR NEPHEW, COOPER

-Katie & Kevin Tsang

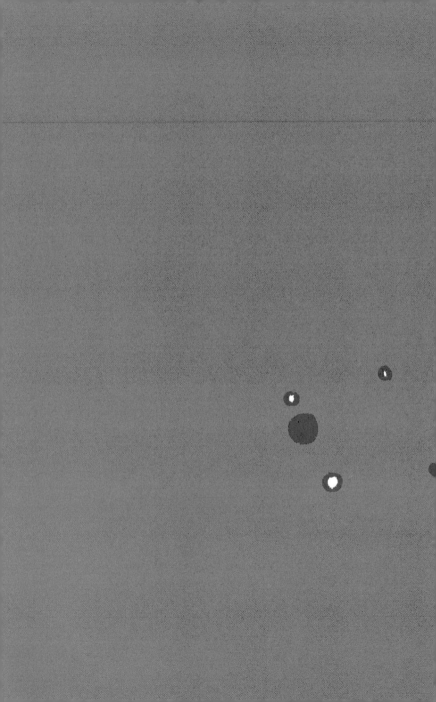

CONTENTS

CHAPTER 1

WHAT COULD BE WORSE THAN SHARKS?

My name is **Sam Wu**, and I am <u>**NOT**</u> afraid of the dark. Or sharks. Or ghosts.

You might be wondering why I'm listing all the things I'm <u>**NOT**</u> afraid of.

It's because lately I've had to prove just how very brave I am.

And let me tell you, proving how brave you are is **HARD WORK**.

Only the bravest can do it, really.

Most recently, I had to prove I wasn't afraid

of sharks. This is because **Ralph Philip Zinkerman the Third**, who is the **WORST PERSON IN THE WHOLE UNIVERSE**, invited me to his birthday party. At the beach. And as everybody knows, the beach is home of the sharks. Ralph was basically inviting me to Certain Doom.

But Ralph underestimated just how brave I am (as usual). With the help of my **two best friends**, Zoe and Bernard, and a trusty chili-pepper belt (it made sense at the time), we were able to outsmart the sharks *and* Ralph. I even saved Ralph's grandpa from getting **eaten** by a shark![1]

---

[1] This may not be exactly what happened, but you get the idea. I was very brave and was the hero of the birthday party. I proved that sharks don't scare me.

Before the sharks, well, there was this whole situation with a ghost in my house. And my pet snake, Fang, who is **VERY** dangerous, went missing. We still think that maybe the ghost and Fang were working together.

At least I still think that. Bernard tells me that we have **no evidence**.

Bernard might be the smartest kid I know, but he doesn't know *everything*. He didn't even know what **SPACE BLASTERS** was until I told him about it.

And **EVERYONE** knows about **SPACE BLASTERS!** It's the very best show in the **universe**. It's my favorite thing on TV. If I could do anything, I'd be a member of the crew on TUBS, which stands for The Universe's Best Spaceship. It is led by Captain Jane and Spaceman Jack and their alien friend, Five-Eyed Frank. They go on all kinds of adventures and aren't scared of **anything**.

Anyway, the lessons I've learned from **SPACE BLASTERS**, ghosts, AND sharks were all just to prepare me for the scariest thing I'll ever encounter. My greatest challenge yet.

THE DARK !/!!

CHAPTER 2

WORSE THAN BEING ZAPPED THROUGH A WORMHOLE

It all started when my friend Bernard came up to me at school with a glum expression. It was the Friday before fall break, so he should have looked happy. (I know I was happy to have a week of **NO SCHOOL!**)

"Guess what?" he said.

"What?" I replied. "You look sadder than an alien zapped twice through a wormhole."

"It's even worse than that," he said, still

frowning. I was glad that Bernard had started watching **SPACE BLASTERS**, so he **TOTALLY** got the wormhole reference.

"Worse? What could be worse than that?"

"Being zapped *four* times," chimed in Zoe. She had also started watching the show. "And then being **VAPORIZED!**"

"Okay, okay. Fine. There are worse things," I said quickly. Zoe really liked the show. She had caught up on all the old episodes and had even got her brothers and sisters to watch it with her. "We can probably assume Bernard isn't going to be zapped or vaporized."

"Or **IS** he?" Zoe said in a **spooky** voice. "Stranger things have happened in space!"

Captain Jane always says that on
SPACE BLASTERS.

I gave her a high five for that one.

"YOU GUYS.
I HAVE TO GO
CAMPING!"

Bernard wailed.

"In the WOODS!"

I'm glad it's Bernard and totally NOT me!!

Oh. That *was* worse than
being zapped twice through a
wormhole.

✶ ✶✶

We met again at lunch to strategize, in our usual
meeting spot by the fence.

"It won't be that bad . . ." I said unconvincingly.

"BEARS, SAM! BEARS! Just think of
the bears!" Bernard said.

7

"And the bugs," added Zoe, wrinkling her nose. Then, as an afterthought. "I don't mind bugs, actually."

"Maybe you'll have fun?" I said, still trying to be enthusiastic for Bernard's sake. "Think of it like an **adventure**."

"Remember all the research we did on sharks?" Bernard said.

I nodded. "But there won't be sharks in the woods, Bernard."[2]

---

[2] I was *pretty* sure about this, but then again you can never be too careful.

"Well, bears are basically the sharks of the woods. They don't have any natural predators. **JUST. LIKE. SHARKS.**"

"Maybe they'll be hibernating!" I said.

"They hibernate in the **winter**. Does it **LOOK** like winter right now?" said Bernard, pointing at the sun.

It is never a good idea to try to out-fact Bernard.

"I think camping sounds kind of cool," said Zoe. "I went once with my family when I was little."

"But you had your brothers and sisters to play with," Bernard pointed out. "It'll just be me and my dad. And the '**great outdoors**,' as he calls it."

Bernard lives with his dad. His mom lives

9

somewhere else, and sometimes he goes to stay with her.

I patted Bernard on the back. "You can do it," I said. "**I believe in you**."

This is what Spaceman Jack always says to a crewmember when they have to do something they don't want to do.

"I'd go with you if I could," I added, feeling especially Spaceman Jack-ish. He is my favorite character on **SPACE BLASTERS**.

"I would go, too!" said Zoe.

"You would?" Bernard's eyes were huge. "Even with the risk of bears? And poison ivy?"

I nodded. "Of course I would. That's what friends are for." I said this thinking that there was no way I'd have to go with him.[3]

I WAS WRONG.

---

[3] Not a lie, but a friendly fib to make my friend feel better. Like when your mom says that getting the flu shot won't hurt, even though you both know that it will.

CHAPTER 3

SURPRISE FROM HONG KONG

When I got home from school that day, there was a surprise waiting for me.

But **NOT** the fun kind, like a present. Or a surprise new episode of **SPACE BLASTERS**.

It was my cousin Stanley from Hong Kong.

And he was staying in **MY ROOM**. For **TWO WEEKS!**

Stanley is only two years older than me, but he thinks he's a teenager.

"What's happening, little cuz?" he said, sitting on **MY** bed.

"I'm not little," I said. "Please get off my bed."

"Your mom says it is *my* bed while I'm here," he said. "That's your bed." He pointed to a pillow and blankets **on the floor**.

And then, just when I thought things couldn't get any worse, Stanley went across my room, opened Fang's cage, **AND PICKED FANG UP**.

"Who is this little guy?" he said.

"Put down Fang! He's **VERY** dangerous," I said in my most serious voice, so that Stanley would understand the current danger he was in. "And he's not little, either!"

"This baby snake's dangerous? You should see the snakes in Hong Kong. Pythons that are bigger than you."

"Fang is **NOT** a baby," I said. I wanted to grab Fang out of Stanley's hands, but I wasn't sure how to do that without making Fang angry. No matter what Stanley said, Fang is **dangerous**. Only the bravest people can handle him. Like me. And occasionally my sister, Lucy. "I've been to Hong Kong. And I never saw a snake bigger than me—or Fang!"

I've never actually seen **ANY** snakes in Hong Kong, but I didn't need to share that detail.

13

I stormed out of my room and went to find my mom in the kitchen. She was on the phone speaking Cantonese.

"Mom!" I knocked on the table in front of her to get her attention. "**MOM!**"

She ignored me and carried on. "He arrived safe and sound," she said. She must have been talking to Stanley's parents in Hong Kong. "We're so glad to have him here."

I stuck my tongue out.

My mom gave me a **mom glare**, which is significantly worse than a normal glare. "Stop that!" she mouthed.

I sat down next to her at the table and kicked the floor. I couldn't believe that my mom was making me give up my bed for Stanley!

My little sister, Lucy, came running in, her

cat, Butterbutt, in her arms.

"STANLEY'S HERE!
Stanley's here!" Lucy
shouted, spinning
around.

"Why are you so
excited about it?"
I said.

"I like Stanley! And he
brought me **sweets** from
Hong Kong."

I thought it would take more than sweets
to bribe Lucy, but apparently I was wrong.

"**What kind of sweets?**" I asked
grudgingly. Lucy held out a sticky hand with
a small wrapped sweet in it.

"Here!" she said.

I popped it in my mouth. I hate to admit it, but it was delicious.

It tasted like lychee. Which is my favorite fruit. It's a fruit from Asia that tastes **AMAZING**. It's sort of like a cherry, if a cherry had a shell. It has three layers—the bumpy red outside that you peel, the white fruit inside that you eat, and a big brown seed in the middle.

"Thank you," I said with my mouth full of lychee candy. I wondered if Stanley had any more. That would be the only good thing about him coming to stay with us.

"Sam! What are you doing pouting and **kicking the floor?**" my mom said as she hung up the phone. "You know better than that."

"Why is Stanley here?" I demanded. "And why is he staying in my room? In my **BED?**"

"He's here because he has a new baby brother and sister, and his parents need some time to get the twins settled. And he's here because he's family, and **family is always welcome**."

Twins! I looked at Lucy and tried to imagine two of her.

"But why is he in *my* room?"

My mom sighed. "Because he's your cousin, Sam. And you two will have fun! Why don't you show him your **SPACE BLASTERS** cards or something?"

"Why can't he stay in the garage? Or on the roof?"

"**WU GABO!**"[4] Mom shouted. "Get upstairs and be nice to your cousin. Right now."

I marched up the stairs, back to my room. It wasn't as if I had a choice in the matter.

At least I didn't have to go camping.

---

[4] Wu Gabo is my Chinese name, and my mom only uses it when she's being very serious.

CHAPTER 4

BAD NEWS FROM THE FUTURE

The next morning at breakfast, everyone kept asking Stanley questions. You would have thought he was the most interesting person in **the _whole_ universe**.

My dad laughed at all his dumb jokes.

My mom complimented him on his hair.

Lucy wanted to sit next to him.

And Na-Na, my grandma who lives with us, gave him extra congee![5]

---

[5] Congee is my favorite breakfast food. It's a rice porridge. And it's delicious.

Even Butterbutt climbed on his lap! And Butterbutt only likes Lucy.

If they all liked Stanley so much, why couldn't he sleep in **THEIR** rooms? Or not-sleep, I should say. Stanley was up all last night because of something called "jet lag,"

which apparently means when you fly across the world your body doesn't know what time it is. He told me about it in his typical know-it-all way. Even though I've been on airplanes, too. And a **real spaceship** at the Space Museum.[6]

"If Spaceman Jack can travel at warp speed and not get jet lag, I don't understand why you got it from just going on an airplane," I said after about a million hours of him telling me about all the things he does in Hong Kong and how cool his life is there. Who cares that they have the most awesome arcades in the world? Or that Stanley supposedly has a top score on a **bajillion** of the games?

---

[6] Although that didn't end well. But that's not important to this story.

Or that at this amusement park called Ocean Park, you can ride roller coasters, watch pandas, and see sharks?[7]

"It's as if I'm from the future," Stanley went on. "I left on Saturday and arrived here on Friday. I'm basically a **time traveler**."

"You just took a flight," I grumbled. "No big deal." It wasn't as if he'd gone on a spaceship.[7] Then I'd be impressed. Maybe.

"Hey, Sam," Stanley said in between bites of congee. "Remember when you first came to Hong Kong and there was a typhoon[8], and you were so scared?"

"I was **NOT**," I said with a scowl.

"That typhoon wasn't even a big one. We had an even bigger typhoon after you left! It made our whole apartment building shake."

---

[7] Which, as you know, I am definitely not afraid of.
[8] A typhoon is a huge storm. They can be scary if you are the type of person who is afraid of things. Which I am not.

"You should see the storms on **SPACE BLASTERS**," I said. "Spaceman Jack and Captain Jane have to fly through them while blasting evil alien lords. Way harder than just hiding in your apartment building."

"Is **SPACE BLASTERS** that show you kept talking about last night? The one that is like *Star Wars*?"

"It's *not* like *Star Wars*," I scoffed. "Everyone knows **SPACE BLASTERS** is way better."

"Cool," said Stanley. "Maybe after

23

breakfast you could show me an episode or two."

I was **so surprised** that I almost dropped my congee spoon.

Just as we finished breakfast, the phone rang. My dad answered it.

"Oh hello, Bill! How are you?"

I figured Bill was one of Dad's friends or a neighbor or something and went into the living

room to show Stanley my SPACE BLASTERS cards and to explain to him how the SPACE BLASTERS universe works. Finally something that I could explain to him!

"Camping? Why, that sounds great! I'm sure

Sam would love to go," said my dad.

I froze in my tracks.

What?

My dad went on, "The only thing is, we've got his cousin Stanley here with us."

Whew! Who would have thought I'd be saved by Stanley, of all people?

But then Stanley turned to my mom. "I love camping!" he said. "I'm actually **a camping pro**."

Oh no.

"Hold on a second, Bill," said my dad. He turned to my mom and Stanley. "Would you like to go camping, Stanley?"

"**I'd love to!**" said Stanley.

No, no, no. This was not good.

"Can I go, too?" Lucy chimed in. "I'll bring Butterbutt!"

"**NO!**" everyone said at the same time. We all knew Butterbutt plus Lucy plus the outdoors was a recipe for **disaster**.

"I never get to do anything," Lucy grumbled. "Butterbutt and I will just camp in the back garden then, won't we, Butterbutt?"

Butterbutt yowled in reply.

"Maybe camping isn't a great idea for any of us," I suggested hopefully, but nobody was listening to me.

My dad put the phone back up to his ear. "Bill, that would be great. Thanks so much. I'm sure they'll have a wonderful time."

He hung up and turned to me with a huge smile.

"**GREAT** news! You and Stanley are going camping with Bernard and his dad!"

This was, in fact, <u>**NOT**</u> great news.

Camping would have been **terrible** on its own (I remembered everything Bernard had said about bears)—and now I had to go with Stanley!

The only solution was to stop this doomed camping trip before it had even started.

"I'll be right back!" I called as I ran out of the door, hopped on Two-Wheel **TUBS**[9], and pedaled off to fix this disaster.

---

[9] Two-Wheel TUBS is the name of my bike. It's named after The Universe's Best Spaceship on SPACE BLASTERS, but I added the "Two-Wheel" so people know it's a bike.

CHAPTER 5

BOOKS WON'T
SAVE YOU FROM BEARS

Bernard lives over the river on the other side of town, but I biked there so fast it was like I was traveling at **light speed**.

I ran up his driveway and rang the doorbell five times to let Bernard and his dad know that I was there on very urgent business.

Bernard's dad answered the door. He looked as if he had just come *back* from a camping trip. During which he'd wrestled and swallowed a bear.

This is actually how he always looks. Bernard's dad is practically a **giant**—he has a big mustache and wears the kinds of clothes that I imagine a lumberjack would wear. And he's <u>**NOT**</u> even a lumberjack!

Bernard says he's a palaeontologist, which I think means he likes to dig up old stuff. I don't know how that is a real job, but grown-ups are **weird**. Once I asked him if he'd ever dug up a dinosaur or a mummy, and instead he showed me

29

a rock with a leaf stuck in it and said it was thousands of years old. I was **NOT** impressed. A **really old rock** is nowhere near as cool as a dinosaur.

"Oh hi, Sam! Did your finger get stuck to the doorbell?" Bernard's dad grinned. "I didn't think I'd see you till tomorrow morning when we pick you up to go camping. I bet you're excited—I know I am. It's going to be great for you kiddos. Getting out into the great outdoors, breathing in all that fresh air, camping under the stars, exploring the wilderness. All that good stuff."

"Hi, Mr. Wilson," I said, ignoring everything he'd just said. "Is Bernard home? It's **VERY IMPORTANT**."

"Is everything all right?"

"It will be," I said seriously.

"Well, okay then. Come on in."

I squeezed past Bernard's dad, ran up the stairs to Bernard's room, and flung open his door. Bernard was reading on his bed.

"We have **_got_** to get out of camping," I said breathlessly.

✦ ✦✦

Ten minutes later, I'd explained to Bernard that, actually, he was right, and that camping was a terrible idea.

"Remember the **bears**, Bernard? And the poison ivy? And what about wolves? It's going to be too risky. We've got to stop it. We're the only ones brave enough."

Bernard frowned. "Brave enough to stop the camping trip?"

"Exactly! Brave enough to **SAVE** everyone

from certain disaster. Like getting lost in the dark woods and eaten by bears. **OR WORSE.**"

"Or worse?"

I lowered my voice. "Bernard, do you know how dark it is in the woods? **VERY DARK**. Darker than this." I covered Bernard's eyes with my hands.

"Ow! You poked me in the eye!"

I'd done that by accident, but it actually helped to prove my point.

"Imagine if my finger had been a **SHARP THORN** that you'd walked into! Or a **RAMPAGING BAT!**"[10]

"Sam," said Bernard, pushing my hands away from his face. "*You* said camping would be fun. And that you *would* go with me if you could. Well, now you can!"

"And I **WOULD**. But this isn't about you and me, Bernard. It is bigger than us!" That's something Spaceman Jack always says when he's trying to convince Captain Jane to do something.

"What do you mean?" Bernard asked.

_____

[10] I'm not sure if bats rampage, but Bernard didn't need to know that.

I grabbed Bernard by the shoulders and shook him. I'd seen Spaceman Jack do that, too. "**THINK OF THE SHIP, BERNARD!**" I opened my eyes as wide as I could to really get my point across.

"Sam, is this a **SPACE BLASTERS** thing again? You're acting weird."

"I'm only trying to save you, Bernard. It's what friends do."

"I think you just don't want to go camping," said Bernard.

I looked at the bed and saw the cover of the book he'd been reading. It was called *Mountain Man: How to Survive a Bear Encounter*. I held up the book. "Books won't save you from bears, Bernard."

"They might! I've learned lots of stuff in that

34

one. Such as if you see a bear, you should either
(a) try to scare it by making yourself bigger or
(b) play dead."

"THOSE ARE TWO VERY DIFFERENT THINGS, BERNARD! I CAN'T MAKE MYSELF BIGGER AND PLAY DEAD AT THE SAME TIME. I DON'T EVEN THINK I CAN MAKE MYSELF BIGGER."

I was pretty sure I could play dead though. The live mice we feed my pet snake, Fang, do it all the time.

"Listen, Sam, my dad has gone camping loads of times. He gave me this book! And this one!" Bernard held up another book with the title *Camping: Be One With Nature.* "And you know how big my dad is. He won't even have to try to make himself **bigger** if we do see a bear."

He had a point.

"And I've done the math," Bernard added.[11] "Statistically, at least seventy-five percent of us will survive. With you and Stanley coming, that increases our odds!"

HIGHER
CHANCE

STATS:
INCREASE OF ODDS

LOWER
CHANCE

---

[11] Bernard loves math way more than any other kid I've ever met.

"But my chances of **surviving** would be one hundred percent if I didn't go," I said, proud of myself for also knowing how to do math. "And it isn't just about the bears, Bernard." I lowered my voice. "It's the *dark*. Anything could be out there."

"We'll bring flashlights," said Bernard firmly. Then he looked very seriously at me. "And you know that there's no getting out of it if our parents want us to go. So we might as well prepare as much as we can."

He was right.

Our fate was sealed.

We were going camping.

CHAPTER 6

A MILLION ROCKS ON MY BACK

Packing for camping was hard. How *do* you pack for **certain disaster?**

It was even harder because Stanley kept unpacking everything I put in my backpack.

"You don't need your **SPACE BLASTERS** Cards," he said, laughing. "You need rain boots."

"I was just about to pack those," I said, jamming my rain boots in my backpack.

Then I had no space left for anything else.

Stanley laughed again. "You attach them to

the outside of your backpack, like this." He held up his bag to show me.

Stanley had finished packing hours ago. And now he was just criticizing my every move.

He looked at the pile of stuff on my bed again. "You don't need a bag of rice, either."

"What if I get hungry?"

"Bernard's dad will have food," he said. Then he puffed out his chest a bit. "Or I'll catch us a fish! I'm an **expert** at fishing."

"Hmmm," I said, doubtful.

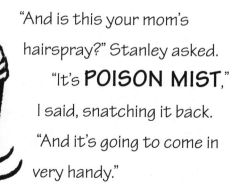

"And is this your mom's hairspray?" Stanley asked. "It's **POISON MIST**," I said, snatching it back. "And it's going to come in very handy."

Stanley just laughed again. And then he ruffled my hair like he was a grown-up and not just two years older than me. "We're going to have the **best time!**"

At least one of us was excited.

✦ ✦✦

The next morning came way too soon.

Not only did I get no sleep thanks to

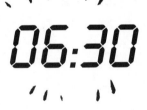

Stanley's snoring, Bernard and his dad arrived early, so I didn't even have time to finish my breakfast.

And everybody knows you should never go into battle on an **empty stomach**.

Stanley of course had been up since dawn because of his stupid "jet lag," so he'd already had three bowls of congee.

"Let's hit the open road!" Bernard's dad yelled from the car as he honked on his horn.

My mom cringed.

"Have fun, Sam," she said. "And **BE GOOD**. No **SPACE BLASTERS** nonsense or ghosts or any of it, okay? Just listen to Bernard's dad. And be nice to Stanley."

"Okay, okay," I said, letting Mom hug me.

"You're going to have the **best time!**" my dad declared.

"If camping's so much fun, how come you aren't coming?" I asked.

My dad scratched the back of his head. "Oh, you know. Someone's got to stay at home and look after things. You have a great time. We'll see you when you get back. And, as your mom said, be nice to Stanley, all right? Don't let me down."

"Okay, okay," I grumbled. My dad ruffled my hair.

I turned and hugged Lucy, who was still in her pajamas. "**Farewell, Lucy,**" I said dramatically. "Take care of Butterbutt and Fang. And say bye to Na-Na for me." Na-Na was still asleep, and waking her up is **even more dangerous** than going camping.

Lucy squirmed out of my hug. "You're only going away for two nights!" she said.

I shook my head. "You're just too young to understand." That's what Spaceman Jack says whenever he doesn't want to tell an alien that **their entire planet** is about to be wiped out by bad guys.

Lucy rolled her eyes. "I understand *everything*." Then she stepped up on to her

tiptoes and whispered in my ear, "You'll be okay!" With a grin, she tapped my backpack. "I snuck something in your bag."

"It isn't Butterbutt, right?" I quickly looked around the kitchen just to make sure. A worse thought occurred to me. "Or Fang?"

Lucy laughed. "No, no, silly." Then she whispered again, "It's my *night-light*. Just in case you need it."

"Oh, I won't," I said breezily. "I'm

NOT

afraid of the dark. But I'll take it anyway, you know, just in *case* anyone else needs it."

The drive to the campsite took **FOREVER**. Bernard's dad let Stanley sit in the front because "he's the guest," and Bernard and I were squished in the back with all the camping gear.

We had a **LOT** of gear. It almost made me feel as if we were going on a space expedition instead of camping. Which I liked a lot.

There aren't bears in space.[12]

Bernard's dad made us listen to weird old-people music for a whole hour. I thought that was bad, but then all we had to listen to was Stanley talk about how much he loves camping and how he goes camping **ALL** the time in Hong Kong and how he's a camping expert.

But I would have stayed in the car forever if it meant never having to go into the woods.

We finally parked and got out of the car, and then it was time to head in.

To the **dark woods**.

The dark, dark woods.

---

[12] Although one time there was an Evil Alien Bear on SPACE BLASTERS. So you never know.

And it was **still daytime!** I couldn't understand how it was so dark when the sun was out. Who knew trees could be so good at making shade?

As we headed through the woods to the campsite, I was sure that my backpack was **WAY** heavier than when I left this morning. It felt like I had a million rocks on my back. I didn't think we were ever going to make it to the campsite.

"Come on, Sammy!" shouted Stanley from ahead of me. He was skipping alongside a stream that led to the campsite like he was in zero gravity.

"Don't call me Sammy!" I shouted back. Or at least I tried to shout. I was too out of breath.

"I'll help you!" he called and skipped back to me.

"I've got it!" I said, hanging on to my backpack straps for dear life.

"I . . . can . . . help!" Stanley said, pulling on the back of my bag.

"Hey, guys," said Bernard.

"I said, **I'VE GOT IT. I CAN CARRY MY OWN BACKPACK. A SPACEMAN ALWAYS CARRIES HIS OWN PACK.**"

"We aren't in space," Stanley said, pulling harder. "Let me help. We'll go faster."

"Guys!" said Bernard.

"**EVERYTHING IS IN SPACE!**" I shouted, and I flung myself forward with all my might, just as Stanley let go of my backpack.

I toppled into the stream.

I shouted.

"Don't worry, Sam!" cried Bernard, jumping in next to me. "I'll save you!"

"**I'LL SAVE THE BAG!**" yelled Stanley, grabbing the backpack off my back.

I suddenly realized that I was on my hands and knees, and not sinking.

Bernard also realized this, as the water only came up to his ankles. Still he helped me up.

My knees were covered in cuts from the rocks in the stream. It hurt, a lot, but I took a deep breath and remembered to be **brave**.

"What's going on back here?" cried Bernard's dad, who had gone on ahead to set up our camp. "You kids are taking forever!"

Then he saw the state of us.

"What happened?"

The three of us exchanged

rapid looks. It would have been easy for me and Bernard to turn on Stanley. **Two against one**. Mr. Wilson would have had no choice but to believe us.

But I heard Captain Jane in my head.

"*A crew always works together, even if they don't always get along.*"

"I tripped and fell," I said. "Stanley saved my bag from getting wet, and Bernard helped me up."

Bernard's dad looked at us suspiciously. "Hmmm, well, be careful, all right? And **stay on the path**. That's the most important thing about hiking in the woods. Staying on the path." He frowned at my scraped knees. "Let's get those knees cleaned up."

I took another deep, extremely brave breath.

My knees were stinging and so were my eyes.

"I'll be okay," I said.

Bernard's dad chuckled. "I know you will, you're a **tough kid**, but it's still a good idea to clean up those scrapes."

I beamed. He was right.

I was tough.

Spaceman Jack would have been proud.

CHAPTER 7

IMPORTANT LIFE SKILLS

Camping was hard work.

When we arrived at the campsite, Bernard's dad made us put up our own tent.

"It's a great skill to have! Something you can't learn in your books, Bernard. You've got to get some **real-life skills**," he said.

"I have plenty of real-life skills," Bernard grumbled. "I know how to swim now and everything!" Bernard had recently learned to swim, and I'd call it more "not-drowning" than swimming, but now didn't seem the time to point that out.

"And now you'll know how to put up a tent," his dad said.

"*I* know how to put up a tent," said Stanley. Of course he did.

"**Big surprise**," I muttered to myself.

"But I'll let you guys try first," Stanley said, smiling at us. I tried to figure out if it was a tricky smile. Like he was **TRYING** to set us up for failure. But no, it was his normal smile. "Bernard's dad is right. It's good to know how to set up a tent."

"Great!" said Bernard's dad. "I'll go and get the rest of the supplies from the car. Bernard and Sam, you guys get that tent set up. Stanley, you supervise."

Before I could protest that I did **NOT** need Stanley to supervise me doing anything, Bernard's dad disappeared into the woods.

If Stanley could set up a tent, surely I could, too. As I said, he's only two years older than me—no matter how much he tries to pretend he's so mature.

"We can do this, Bernard," I said, eyeing the pile of sticks and fabric on the ground that would apparently turn into a tent. Maybe it was like a **magic trick**.

But doing magic tricks is not one of my strengths. I found this out the hard way, during show-and-tell at school when I tried to pull a rabbit out of a hat. Apparently, you need to have a rabbit in the first place if you are going to pull one out of a hat. Who knew?

"Okay!" said Bernard, clapping his hands. "You start."

"Hmmm," I said, circling the "tent." It sure didn't look like a tent. It looked like a **deflated hot-air balloon**. "Bernard! You should get inside and hold it up."

He did as I asked.

Ah-ha! Now it looked like a tent.

"Like this?" asked Bernard, his voice muffled beneath the fabric.

"**Perfect!** Just . . . stay like that."

I was pretty impressed with our tent-making skills so far.

"Can I move yet?" asked Bernard.

I had no idea what to do next.

I decided the best thing to do would be to find something else to focus on. We could deal with the tent later.

"We should actually survey the area before we set up our tent," I said with as much authority as I could muster. "That's what Spaceman Jack and Captain Jane do when they land on a new planet. Just to make sure there aren't any **enemies** hiding nearby."

Stanley frowned. "But Bernard's dad said we should camp here."

"Well, we should check the area just in case," I said.

"In case of what?" asked Stanley, still frowning.

"BEARS!"

shouted Bernard from inside the tent.

"Or aliens!"

I added.

"OR WOLVES!"

yelled Bernard.

"There could be anything, really," I said. "Best to take a good look around to see what we're dealing with."

"I don't know," said Stanley. "I told Bernard's dad I'd supervise setting up the tent."

"And we **WILL** set up the tent! We're already halfway there." I gestured at Bernard holding up the tent and I leaned toward Stanley. "Think how much more impressed Bernard's dad will be when we can declare this a safe area to camp."

"I guess," said Stanley, sounding unsure.

"Great!" I said. "Well, let's start looking around."

"What about me?' called Bernard from the tent. "Do I have to stay in here?"

"You're coming with us," I said. "We'll deal with this **tent situation** when we get back."

What I meant was, Stanley could deal with it. After all, I was going to be a spaceman someday—and you don't need to know how to put up a tent in space.

CHAPTER 8

A SUSPICIOUS SNORT

"So what exactly are we looking for?" asked Stanley as we went into the woods.

"Stanley, let us lead the expedition," I said. "We're **experienced** in this kind of thing."

"Yeah!" said Bernard.

"Okay, but I still don't know what I'm looking for."

For someone who said he was a camping expert, Stanley had no idea how to make sure the area was secure. Which I was pretty sure was the first step in camping.

"Well," I said. "First of all, we have to use *all* our senses."

"Maybe not **all** of them," said Bernard. "Probably not taste."

I sighed. "Okay, fine. We have to use *most* of our senses. Do you hear anything?" I cupped my hand behind my ear.

Bernard and Stanley did the same.

I heard the stream going by, and birds chirping, and something else. Something rustling in the bushes. Something **BIG**.

"Do you hear that?" I said, whipping my head around.

I saw Stanley hopping from one foot to the other, making the bushes rustle.

"Stanley! You're being too **loud!**" I said.

"Sorry! I thought I saw a bee. I hate bees." He shuddered.

Interesting. The first thing that Stanley *didn't* like about camping. I pocketed this knowledge for later.

"Bernard, do we have the binoculars?" I asked.

"In my bag. Back at the campsite."

"Well, I guess for now, just look as hard as you can with your eyes." We all stared into the **dark woods**.

"I don't think there's anything here," said Stanley after a minute. "And really, we don't have anything to worry about. *Now,* if we were camping in Hong Kong, we'd have stuff to worry about. Wild pigs, snakes, monkeys, maybe even a tiger."

"I'm really glad we're camping here and not in Hong Kong," said Bernard.

"We still have **PLENTY** to worry about here," I said. "Bears, remember? And wolves?" I gave Stanley a pointed look. "And **BEES**."

Something growled.

64

Bees don't growl.

"**DID YOU HEAR THAT?**" I said.

"Hear what?" said Bernard.

"That growl!" I didn't know how to take on a bear! We had to get out of here right now. I tried to remember what Bernard had said about protecting yourself from a bear. How could I make myself bigger? Or should I play dead?

There was another growl, louder this time. "**I HEARD THAT ONE!**" said Bernard.

I grabbed my poison mist. This was no time to play dead. "**MAKE YOURSELF BIG!**" I yelled.

Something rustled in the bushes in front of me. It crossed my mind that a bear would be too big to hide in these bushes, but I wasn't taking any chances. And maybe it was a sneaky bear! I sprayed my poison mist straight into the bushes. "**I'VE GOT YOU!**" I shouted.

Whatever it was started snorting. And there was something very familiar about this snort . . .

"That's not a bear," said Stanley, as a head popped out of the bushes. "That's another kid."

It wasn't just any kid.

It was Ralph Philip Zinkerman. Of course. He even had his **bow tie** on.

Ralph was rubbing his eyes. "What did you spray at me?" he said, coughing.

"It's **POISON MIST**," I said, avoiding Stanley's gaze. "You're lucky to be alive! And I sprayed you because I thought you were a bear! What are you even doing here?"

"Poison mist?" Ralph sounded genuinely panicked. "**AM I GOING TO DIE?**"

"It's just hairspray," said Stanley. "But here's some water. Sorry about that. Sam acts before he thinks sometimes."

I bristled. "**I WAS PROTECTING US!**" And as Spaceman Jack says, sometimes there is no time to think. You just have to go on instinct.

"You should have seen your face," said Ralph, who managed to snort-laugh even as he splashed water into his eyes. "You were **TERRIFIED**. Typical Scaredy-Cat Sam."

"I was **NOT** afraid,"
I said. "And not nearly as
afraid as you were when
I said I sprayed you with
poison mist."

"Lucky I wasn't a real bear," said
Ralph, ignoring me. "If you sprayed a
real bear with hairspray, it would just
get mad and then rip you to shreds!"

He made a claw with his hands.

I shuddered. I hate to admit it, but
Ralph might have had a point. I'd need to be
better prepared for any future **creature
encounters**.

"Can we change the subject?" asked Bernard.
"You still haven't said what you are doing here,
Ralph. Are you camping by yourself?" Bernard

looked over Ralph's shoulder.

Was he? Ralph couldn't be brave enough to camp on his own. Could he? But then Captain Jane always says you should never underestimate your **enemies**.

"I'm with my parents and my sister," said Ralph. "Zach was supposed to come, but he got the flu."

Zach was one of Ralph's friends who always laughed at Ralph's bad jokes. I suspected that Zach had wisely pretended to have the flu to get out of going camping. I should have thought of that.

Well, at least Regina, Ralph's twin sister, was somewhere here, too. Regina is the opposite of Ralph. She's nice and **not-awful**. I wondered where she was. Then I heard a familiar voice. Two familiar voices. I looked up behind Ralph and saw not just Regina, but Zoe, too!

"**Zoe!**" I waved my arms in the air.

She grinned and ran over to us.

"For the universe!" she said, pumping her arm up in our signature SPACE BLASTERS move.

"For the universe!" Bernard and I said back.

"What are you losers doing?" scoffed Ralph.

"It's from this show **SPACE BLASTERS**," said Regina. My mouth almost fell open. Regina knew about **SPACE BLASTERS**? "Zoe's been telling me about it."

"Well, you look stupid," said Ralph.

Regina laughed. "Ralph is just cranky because his friend Zach couldn't come. But now we've found you guys! This is perfect!"

"It is <u>NOT</u> perfect"

"It is <u>NOT</u> perfect"

Ralph and I said it at the same time. Didn't Regina know that we were sworn enemies?

"There you are!" boomed a voice. It was Bernard's dad. "I've been looking **everywhere**

72

for you all! What did I tell you about wandering away from the path? And the tent still isn't set up."

Ralph looked at Bernard's dad. "**Whoa**," he said, clearly impressed by the fact that Bernard's dad is basically a giant.

"Bill Wilson!" shouted a voice from behind Ralph. "What are the chances?"

"Is that Philip and Felicity Zinkerman?" said Bernard's dad, conveniently forgetting that he was annoyed at us for not listening to him. "What a great surprise!"

Ralph and Regina's parents emerged out of the woods. They looked as if they had stepped out of a **spy movie**. They were both dressed in black and had huge, dark sunglasses on, even though it wasn't sunny in the woods.

"Hello, everyone!" said Ralph and Regina's mom. "How **delightful** to see you, and what a splendid surprise this is! We absolutely must all camp together! How wonderful for the children." She clapped her hands together in excitement.

No!

"NO" Ralph and I yelled out, again in unison. I wondered if being **sworn enemies** meant we were connected in some way. Sometimes this happens on SPACE BLASTERS.

"That's a terrific idea," said Bernard's dad, ignoring our shouts. "I was wondering how I was going to entertain this crew on my own. And now they can all play together."

"WE'RE <u>NOT</u> PLAYING," I said, but nobody was listening to me.

"Mother, Father, we should camp at our *own* campsite," said Ralph.

"Oh, Ralphie, don't you want to camp with your friends?" said his mom.

"These aren't my friends!" Ralph protested. "All my friends are back at home."

"Of course these are your friends! I recognize them from your birthday party. It really just seems meant to be, especially as Zach couldn't come," Ralph's mom cooed. "This is just **splendid!**"

Ralph and I both groaned. Parents never understand how things work. I don't think they remember what being a kid is like at all.

Part of me wanted to stop this **RIGHT NOW**, because the only thing worse than camping would be camping with Stanley and the only thing worse than **THAT** would be camping with Ralph Phillip Zinkerman the Third. But I thought that maybe Zoe and Regina would make up for it.

Plus, I knew I'd be in big trouble if I was rude to Ralph's parents and my mom found out about it. And she would *definitely* find out. She has **super-secret mom powers**.

Bernard and I exchanged a quick look. I nodded, and he nodded back.

"I think it's a good idea," I said loudly.

"You *do*?" said Ralph incredulously.

"Me, too!" said Regina, beaming at me. I smiled back.

"This is great!" said Zoe.

"And I'm Stanley!" declared Stanley. I was surprised he didn't introduce himself as the camping expert.

Ralph's mom looked down at him. "Oh, hello, dear. I thought I didn't recognize you."

"I'm great at camping," he added.

"Well, then it's a good thing we are all joining

forces," said Ralph's dad.

"We've just finished setting up our camp, so do you mind coming to our site?" added Ralph's mom. "It's lovely. **Very close** to a waterfall and a natural cave, apparently."

Didn't they know what slept in **CAVES?**
Bears. **Werewolves**.
Bats. **Monsters**.

Bernard's dad clearly wasn't thinking about all that.
"**It sounds fantastic**," he said. "Come on, kiddos, let's pack up and move camp."

A cave? Why would anyone want to sleep near a <u>CAVE</u>.

CHAPTER 9

HOT DOGS AND MARSHMALLOWS

Ralph and Regina's family had the **fanciest** camping equipment I'd ever seen.

"This is a tent?" I said, staring at what looked like a spaceship.

"It's my spaceship tent," said Ralph smugly. He eyed Stanley. "You seem cool. Even though you're related to Sam. Do you want to come in?"

"This is the **coolest** camping gear I've ever seen!" exclaimed Stanley. "How long did it take you to set up?"

"**Ninety seconds**. And it set itself up. All I had to do was press a button."

Stanley nodded, impressed.

I was half-expecting the spaceship to take off. Maybe it would take Ralph with it.

"Stanley," I said, "you have to help us set up *our* tent, remember?" Stanley might be an annoying cousin, but he's *my* annoying cousin. Ralph couldn't steal him.

"Let me help these guys, and then I'll check out your tent," Stanley said to Ralph.

"You're missing out," said Ralph. Then he held up a **CELL PHONE** and pressed a button. Music started playing from inside his tent.

I gasped. **"YOU HAVE A PHONE?"** I didn't think *anyone* in our class had a phone.

"And a speaker inside the tent," said Ralph smugly, going inside his spaceship tent.

"I have a phone, too," said Regina from next to me. "But I left mine at home. Our parents let Ralph bring his phone because his friend Zach couldn't come."

I couldn't believe it. Ralph had a cell phone. And it looked like a **super high-tech** one, too.

A not-nice feeling went through me.

A feeling that made my stomach hurt and my skin feel tight.

Jealousy.

I wanted a cell phone.

And a spaceship tent that set itself up.

It just **wasn't fair**.

"Have you seen our tent?" Regina went on. "Zoe and I are staying in this one." She pointed to an even bigger tent shaped like a castle. "But I like your tent, Sam. It looks more like what I imagine when I think of camping." She smiled. I tried to smile back, but my face muscles weren't working very well. A common side effect of **extreme jealousy**. Not my proudest moment.

Come on, Sam, I heard Captain Jane in my head. *Be grateful for what you have.*

"Yeah, our tent is **pretty awesome**," I managed.

"Yeah!" said Bernard. "I love our tent!"

"Me, too!" I said, and this time I meant it. And my smile was real. I didn't want Bernard to feel bad. I was lucky to get to share a tent with my best friend.

Even if we had to share it with my cousin Stanley. Which reminded me . . .

"Stanley, this is Zoe and Regina," I said. They waved. "That's Ralph in there." I pointed at the spaceship tent, which was still **blasting music**. "This is my cousin Stanley. He's from Hong Kong."

"Cool!" chorused Zoe and Regina.

Something occurred to me. I turned to Zoe.

"When did you decide to go camping with Regina? You didn't say anything about camping at school on Friday."

"I was always going to sleep over at her house this weekend, and then I suggested that we go camping! Since I knew Bernard was going, I figured you'd end up going, too."

I nodded, impressed at her **superior detective skills**. "Wow," I said.

"Yeah," she said, grinning. "I've learned some stuff from SPACE BLASTERS, too, you know. I just tried to think like Captain Jane."

I couldn't have been more proud.

✦ ✦✦

After we finally got everything set up, Bernard's dad made us a fire.

"This one is for you kids," he said. "You're all mature enough to have your own fire and not fall into it or anything, right?"

We all nodded.

"And I'm right here." He pointed to another fire he'd made nearby. "With Ralph and Regina's parents. So just shout if you need us. But for now . . ." He reached into a bag and pulled out **hot dogs and marshmallows**.

"Hot dogs and marshmallows?" Zoe whispered. "What kind of combination is that?"

"You don't eat them together," Bernard whispered back. "We're having hot dogs for dinner, and marshmallows for dessert! We're going to make **s'mores!**"[13]

---

[13] A s'more is a gooey, delicious dessert made with a marshmallow, a piece of chocolate, and graham crackers.

"I've never had a s'more!" Zoe said, sounding excited. "This is going to be great!"

I grinned. Zoe was right. It was going to be great.

Plus, everybody knows that a **roaring fire** keeps away the monsters in the dark.

Or so I thought.

✦ ✦ ✦

As we sat around the fire, roasting our hot dogs and marshmallows, Stanley started talking. And talking. And talking.

But the surprising thing was, we all wanted to listen to him! He was telling campfire stories and, as much as it pains me to admit it, they were actually really good.

Soon, it was dark **everywhere** but closest to the fire. Everyone's faces looked different in the firelight. I knew that Bernard's dad and Ralph and Regina's parents were nearby, but there was **NO WAY** I would cross the dark to get from our fire to their fire. Who knew what could get me?

Stanley, apparently.

"Do you know what comes out at night?" he said in a spooky voice, shining a flashlight under his face.

"Owls," said Bernard. He had one of his books in his lap and was flipping through it with his own flashlight.

"And bats!" said Regina.

"That's right, Regina," said Stanley. "But not just any bats . . . **VAMPIRE BATS!**"

We all shuddered.

"Normal bats also come out at night," said Bernard.

"Well, this story isn't about normal bats," said Stanley in his usual voice. "It's about ... **VAMPIRE BATS**. And werewolves! And all the things that can get you in the dark." ★

Suddenly, I thought I heard a howl out in the night.

"Stop it, Ralph," I said. Because it had to have been him. He was sitting across the fire from me in the direction I'd heard the **howl**.

Ralph looked up from his phone. "What are you talking about, Sam Wu-ser?"

"I heard you! Howling. Stop trying to scare me. It won't work."

HOWL!

I expected Ralph to laugh or at least to snort, but instead his eyes got big.

"I didn't howl," he said. "That was one of you!"

We all looked at each other.

"Anyway," said Stanley, "as I was saying, there are a lot of things that can get you in the dark. It isn't just the **werewolves** and **vampires** you have to worry about. Did you know that snakes come out at night, too?"

91

"Of course we know that," said Zoe.

"Sam has a **pet snake**, remember?"

"Yeah!" I said. But I didn't know that snakes came out at night. As far as I could tell, Fang slept all the time. I realized, if he was awake at night, I wouldn't even know, because I'd be sleeping.

I should have known Fang could be sneaky like that.

"If a snake comes to our camp, Sam will know what to do," Regina added confidently. "He brought his pet snake to class and everything." She smiled at me. At least I think she smiled at me. It was hard to tell in the dark.

"THERE WON'T BE ANY

SNAKES," Ralph said loudly.

I remembered that when I brought
Fang to class, Ralph had stood at the very
back of the classroom. I wondered if he was
afraid of snakes. Not that I'd blame him. Only
the **VERY** bravest people are <u>**NOT**</u> afraid of
snakes. Like me.

Stanley sighed loudly. "As I was saying, it
isn't just snakes, werewolves, and vampires you
have to worry about at night. There are other
things, too."

"Like what?" asked Zoe. She sounded skeptical.

"Yeah, like what?" asked Bernard. He sounded
less skeptical and more scared. He'd even put his
book down.

93

"In the deepest, **darkest** part of the woods, there is a creature waiting to come out. It waits till it is so dark that nobody can see it . . . and then . . ."

"**ALIENS!**" shouted Ralph.

"What?" We all turned to him.

"That's a good guess, but it isn't what I was going to say," said Stanley.

"No! There's been a REAL alien sighting," Ralph said. "Near us!"

I dropped my marshmallow in the fire.

ALIENS?

"What are you talking about?" said Regina.

"Look," said Ralph, flashing his phone at us. "Zach just messaged me. There have been UFO sightings tonight. **VERY CLOSE TO US.**"

Bernard looked at me. "Sam, what kind of

aliens do you think they are?" he said, sounding
panicked. "Do you think they are nice aliens like
Five-Eyed Frank from **SPACE BLASTERS** ?"

"Or evil aliens like the ones that live on
Planet Doom?" said Zoe.

"What if it's the Evil Shark Lord in his
spaceship?" Bernard went on. "Or the Ghost
King? **WHAT IF THEY ARE WORKING
TOGETHER?**"

CHAPTER 10

A VERY SERIOUS SITUATION

I was overwhelmed with the possibilities. But I knew I had to stay **focused**. Captain Jane says a good captain never shows fear. And Spaceman Jack says half of being brave is pretending to be brave. I could do this.

I held up my hands. "Everyone needs to stay calm," I said.

"I am calm," said Regina.

"Okay, well everyone else. We need to stay calm and get more information. We can't

96

prepare for an alien attack if we don't know what kind of alien it is."

"**AN ALIEN ATTACK?**" said Zoe.

"They might be friendly," I said. "But we should prepare for the worst."

I looked at Ralph. I didn't like it, but if we were going to defeat the aliens we would have to work together for the greater good.

"**Commander Ralph**," I said. "We need more information."

Ralph stared at me for a long moment across the campfire. I could tell he was debating whether or not to make fun of me. But then he spoke. "Sam, you're going to want to look at this."

He stood up and brought his phone to me.

I stared at the screen.

I had no idea what I was looking at. It was kind of like a map.

"What is this?" I asked.

Stanley peered over my shoulder. "Is that a map? I'm **GREAT** at reading maps." He grabbed the phone and studied it.

Then he looked up, his face pale.

"Ralph's right," Stanley said. "This is showing all kinds of **UFO activity**. Right above where we are."

"What's a UFO again?" asked Regina.

"Unidentified Flying Object," I said. "Which almost definitely one hundred percent means aliens."

"That math doesn't make sense, Sam," said Bernard, frowning.

"*Aliens* don't always make sense," I said.

Bernard nodded. "You're right, there."

"Any other information, Commander Ralph?" I asked.

Ralph shook his head. "No. And stop calling me Commander Ralph."

"**THIS IS A VERY SERIOUS SITUATION**," I said. "We can only defeat the aliens if—"

"We don't even know if it really is aliens,"
interrupted Zoe.

"Okay, we can only defeat *whatever* it is, out
there in the dark, if we're organized. If we're
ready. We can't just be kids out here. We have
to be more."

Ralph rolled his eyes. "I guess I'm commander,
then."

"If Ralph's a commander, what am I?" asked
Bernard.

"**Chief Research Officer**, obviously," I said.
Bernard beamed.

"What about me?" asked Zoe, hopping in place.

"General Zoe, exploration leader."

She grinned.

"This is so much fun!" said Regina.

"Who do I get to be?"

"Admiral Regina."

"Awesome!" said Regina.

"And me?" asked Stanley.

"Colonel Stanley, **camping expert**. Visiting from the Hong Kong team."

Stanley gave me a high-five.

"And what does that make you?" said Ralph.

"Spaceman Sam, I guess," I said.

"No," said Regina. "You're Captain Sam."

I looked at Zoe and Bernard, who nodded. I knew I'd always be a spaceman in my heart, but for this mission, I'd be the captain. Someone had to do it. And I figured I was brave enough.

Just then, there was **another** howl.

HOWL

101

I did my best to put on a brave voice.

"Commander Ralph, did you hear that one?"

Ralph nodded.

"I heard it, too," said Zoe.

We all moved a little closer to the fire.

"So let me get this straight," said Bernard. "We've got aliens to worry about, **plus** whatever is howling in the woods?"

"And all of the other creatures that come out at night," said Stanley.

"Regina, what if the zombie werewolf followed us here?" blurted Ralph.

"**WHAT?!**" the rest of us cried out. Then I remembered.

102

Regina had once said that she and Ralph
thought there was a **zombie werewolf**
haunting their basement.

"It couldn't have followed us," said Regina,
but even she sounded unsure.

"Anything is possible," I said, trying to
keep a steady voice. "I know that from
SPACE BLASTERS."

"Hold on," said Zoe, crossing her arms. "So
what exactly are we worried about? Is it the
zombie werewolf, the aliens, or all the things
Stanley listed?"

"**ALL OF THEM!**" burst out Bernard.
"Don't you see? In the dark, it could be anything.
We have to be prepared for **ANYTHING
AND EVERYTHING.**"

"Chief Research Officer Bernard is right,

as usual," I said, feeling a lot like that was something Spaceman Jack would say about Captain Jane.

"These names are dumb," said Ralph, rolling his eyes, but then his phone beeped again. He looked up at me. "**Another** alien sighting," he said seriously.

beep

"Thank you, Commander Ralph," I said. This time, Ralph didn't say the names were dumb. I took a deep breath and made a decision. "We have to tell the grown-ups."

CHAPTER 11

NO MAN'S LAND

"But our parents are practically across the **whole forest!**" Bernard wailed.

"No they aren't," said Zoe. "They are right there. I can see your dad." She pointed.

"Yeah, but in between us and them is . . . *no man's land*," said Stanley. He gestured at the expanse of darkness between us. "And remember what I said about the creature that comes in the dark . . . "

We all shivered. Zoe scooted closer to the fire.

"What's no man's land?" asked Bernard.

I'd heard it on **SPACE BLASTERS** but couldn't remember what it meant.

Stanley pointed his flashlight in our faces.

"It means **ANYTHING** could happen there. It isn't our territory. And it isn't where the adults are, either. It belongs to **THE DARK**."

We all stared at the dark no man's land. The grown-ups seemed even farther away than they had a second ago. But I could still hear them. They were laughing.

They had **NO IDEA** how much possible danger we were all in.

Typical grown-ups.

"Couldn't Ralph use his phone to call them?" asked Regina. "So we can all stay by the fire?"

"Brilliant idea, Admiral," I said. I looked at Ralph.

Ralph sighed as if we'd asked him to climb a **mountain** or something, but finally he pressed a button on his phone and held it to his ear.

We all waited.

"No answer," he said.

"Maybe we could yell for them?" said Regina.

I shook my head. "No, yelling is for emergencies only."

"Isn't this an emergency?" asked Bernard.

"ALIENS, WEREWOLVES, WHATEVER CREEPY THINGS

Stanley keeps talking about?"

"We have nothing confirmed," I said. "And if we yell, and they come over, and there isn't anything here . . . well, you know how adults are."

"They'll tell us we're being silly and make us go to sleep," said Ralph knowingly.

"Exactly," I said. I still couldn't get over how weird it was that Ralph and I kept having the same thoughts. Especially because he's so evil! But I guess in times of crisis, you have to focus on the **greater evil**. Like alien invasions and werewolves and . . . the scary *thing* Stanley kept mentioning.

"We'll stay calm. So they **HAVE TO** take us seriously," I said, remembering what had happened when I told my own parents about the ghost in our house. They accused me of watching too many episodes of **SPACE BLASTERS** and told me not to listen to everything Na-Na said. Both of which are impossible. There's no such thing as too many **SPACE BLASTERS** episodes, and trust me, when Na-Na wants you to listen to her, you listen to her. "We need to tell them about the alien sightings."

Everyone nodded.

"So . . . who is going to go over there?" asked Zoe.

Everyone looked around at each other.

"Not me," said Bernard. "I've got to stay here and do my job. Which is research." He turned his flashlight on his book again, looking engrossed.

I was impressed but **not** surprised by how seriously he was taking his role as Chief Research Officer.

"What book is that anyway?" asked Regina.

Bernard held it up. "*Nature Survival Guide: 1,000 Deadly Things in the Woods and How to Avoid Them.* I got it at the library," he said.

Regina's eyes got huge. "Yep, that job seems **pretty important**."

"I'm going to stay here by our fire," said Zoe.

"Wait. Aren't you General Zoe, **exploration leader?**" asked Ralph. "This seems like the perfect job for you."

Zoe shook her head back and forth so fast her ponytail almost smacked me in the face. "I explore by daylight," she said firmly. "No point in exploring when you can't see anything."

Zoe had a good point.

"It's just walking over to our parents— what's the big deal?" asked Ralph.

"You go then, if it is no big deal," said Zoe.

Ralph swallowed. "I would, but shouldn't our **fearless captain** go?"

He said this in a very sarcastic Ralph way,

111

and I could tell by the way he said "fearless" and "captain" that he meant the opposite. Like "very afraid" "not-captain." And just when I was starting to like Ralph. I'd even made him our commander!

But he was right. I **wished** I had thought this through before I suggested that someone should go across no man's land.

"Ralph's right. I'll go and tell the grown-ups."

"You shouldn't go alone," said Regina. "I'll go with you. That's something an admiral would do, right?"

"Right!" I said, feeling relieved. I turned to Stanley. "Colonel Stanley, can I leave you in charge?"

Stanley nodded. "I thought I was already in charge," he said. "I'm the oldest, remember?"

I wanted to argue with him, but there wasn't time. "Well, continue on," I said.

I looked at Regina. "**Are you ready?**"

She turned on her flashlight. "I'm ready."

"Then let's go."

"Safe travels, Captain," said Bernard, saluting me.

"We're going to be able to see them the **WHOLE TIME!**" said Ralph with a snort.

"Ralph, stop sabotaging the mission!" said Regina. "Are you with us or not?"

Ralph made a frustrated horse-like sound. "Fine," he said. "Good luck with the mission. But only because my sister is going with you."

It was the best I was going to get.

I flung my hand up in the air.

"**For the universe!**" I shouted.

"For the universe!" cried everyone else.

Except Ralph. But at least he put his hand up

in the air.

CHAPTER 12

INTO THE DARK

Regina and I stepped into the dark.

She shined her flashlight ahead of us.

"We should walk side by side," I said. "So we know if one of us is grabbed from behind."

"Okay," she said.

"And we have to go quickly, but also carefully."

"Got it."

We walked in silence. I tried very hard to be brave. It was scary in the dark. Thankfully the grown-up's fire was getting closer.

And then disaster.

The flashlight went out.

"ARGH!" I yelled. I wanted to run, but I knew I couldn't just abandon Admiral Regina.

"Ahh!" cried Regina. "There's something in my hair!"

I reached out into the dark to help Regina and something scratched my arm!

We had to make an escape. **"COME ON!"** I said, pulling her by the hand and running toward the grown-ups by their fire. No time to be careful. Only speed mattered now.

"Keep going!" Zoe shouted from behind us.

We were so close. Just a few more steps. And then finally we reached the grown-ups.

"Oh, hello, darlings," said Ralph and Regina's mom. She was wearing a fancy coat and pearls.

"Are you having fun?"

"There's something out there!" I cried.

"Out where?" she said. She was remarkably calm.

"OUT THERE. IN NO MAN'S LAND," I said, pointing behind us. **"IT TRIED TO GET US."**

"No man's land, hey?" said Bernard's dad. "I've always been impressed by your imagination, Sam."

"No! I'm not imagining things. Tell them, Regina!"

"It's true, Mom," said Regina, her eyes wide. "We came over here to tell you about the aliens—"

"The aliens!" interrupted her dad with a snort. "Did the aliens try to **GET** you?"

"We don't know what it was!" I said. "But we know that *something* tried to get us and that there are **DEFINITELY** alien sightings. Near us." I tried to make my voice as serious as possible. "I'm not sure if the two are connected, but it might not be safe for us here."

The grown-ups all exchanged a look.

It was a look I knew well.

It meant that they one hundred percent didn't take us seriously.

"There is something **RIGHT** there!" I said, pointing into the dark. "It might have even used magic powers to turn off Regina's flashlight."

"I'll check it out," sighed Bernard's dad, standing up. I was glad he was so big.

He walked over to where we had come from. I took a deep breath.

"**Be careful**, Mr. Wilson!" I cried out.

"Kids, looks like you just ran into a branch," he said, pointing his own flashlight at a tree. "See here?"

119

He was right. It was just a branch. A branch with lots of twigs that looked like fingers.

"I was wondering how you got leaves in your hair," said Regina's mom, brushing them off her.

"But that doesn't explain the **aliens!**" I said. "Which is what we came over to tell you in the first place. Or why Regina's flashlight went out! What if the aliens knew there was a branch there so they used their alien powers to turn off the flashlight right at the moment we ran into it!"

"Where is all this alien talk coming from?" asked Regina's mom.

"Sam is a big fan of a show called SPACE BLASTERS," said Bernard's dad. "It's got all sorts of aliens in it. Isn't that right, Sam?"

"That's why I know we have to take this alien

threat **seriously!**"

The adults exchanged another look.

"Mom, Dad, Sam's right," said Regina. "We saw reports of aliens on Ralph's phone!"

"Is he using data for the internet out here? I told him not to," said their dad. "We said he could use it for games and music only."

"I think you guys might be a little hopped up on sugar from all those marshmallows," said Bernard's dad. "And it's getting pretty late. Probably time for you guys to call it a night."

"BUT THE ALIENS!"

Regina and I cried out.

121

Mr. Wilson squatted down next to us. "Sam, would I let anything **bad** happen to you or Bernard? Or Zoe or any of you kids?"

"Mr. Wilson, all I know about aliens is that you never know what to expect. And I don't know if being a palaeontologist has prepared you for an alien encounter." A thought occurred to me. "Unless you've ever dug up alien bones?"

Bernard's dad rubbed my head. "Can't say that I have, Sam. But I do know that you kids will be fine tonight. Aliens or no aliens, all right?"

I don't know why he thought that would be reassuring. If there was an alien attack, we definitely would **not** be fine.

But I knew this battle was lost. I'd tried my best, and failed my crew.

"All right, Mr. Wilson," I said.

"But just in case, we'll make sure all the flashlights are working, okay? And don't forget, we'll be in tents right next to you. You've got **nothing** to worry about."

I knew then that it would be up to me and the crew to save us all.

CHAPTER 13

A LONG NIGHT

Bernard's dad walked Regina and me back across no man's land. I felt a lot safer with him next to us. And the walk seemed to take way less time than it had coming over.

"Did they tell you about the **aliens**, Dad?" asked Bernard, hopping up and down.

"They did, and I told them what I'm about to tell you. You kids have nothing to worry about. There aren't any aliens here."

"But, Mr Wilson! On Ralph's phone it said

there were!" said Stanley.

"I think that camping is no place for a phone," said Bernard's dad. "You've got yourselves all worked up. And now it's time for bed."

We should have known that the grown-ups wouldn't believe us. They never do.

"But, Dad!" said Bernard.

"I said, it's **time for bed**."

There was no arguing there.

✦ ✦ ✦

Getting ready for bed at home is usually pretty boring. Getting ready for "bed" while camping is a whole other story.

First we brushed our teeth **OUTSIDE**. And spat in the bushes!

Then we took turns to go into different bushes a little farther away to "do our business," as

Bernard's dad called it. There were proper toilets nearby apparently, but nobody wanted to go that far. **_Especially_** not in the dark.

After that, we put on our pajamas inside our tent, which was practically impossible to do because our tent was so small. Bernard kept falling over and Stanley kept getting in my way and I **accidentally** elbowed him in the nose. He didn't even get annoyed at me, just rubbed his nose and said it wasn't my fault.

I'm pretty sure Ralph had plenty of space in his **giant** spaceship tent.

Then Bernard's dad threw dirt on the fire to put it out for the night. "Fire safety," he said. "But be careful, it'll be hot for a while." It was still glowing a little, which I appreciated.

Finally, it was time for bed.

I have to admit, I was pretty impressed that Ralph was sleeping in his own tent by himself. Especially considering all our new intel.[14]

Before I went into my tent for the night, I poked my head into Ralph's tent. Just to check on him, like a good captain should. It looked **AMAZING** in there! He had a lantern and an inflatable mattress! No wonder he was okay about sleeping by himself. But still, being the captain, I knew I should make sure he was fine.

---

[14] Intel is short for intelligence. It's what the SPACE BLASTERS crew say when they have new information. Like ALIEN information.

127

"Commander Ralph," I said.

Ralph sat up and rolled his eyes. "What do you want, Sam? You can knock off the stupid SPACE BLASTERS talk now."

I wanted to leave right then, but I had gone in there with a mission, and I wasn't going to leave till the job was done.

"I just was checking that you'll be okay by yourself?" I said in my best captain voice.

"Of course. I'm **not** scared like some people might be," Ralph said, and snorted knowingly. "Have fun sharing your tiny tent with not just one but TWO other people."

"There's safety in numbers," I said with a shrug. "That's just a fact."

"Well, I'm perfectly fine."

"Even with the zombie werewolf on the loose?"

Ralph frowned and looked away. "I don't want to talk about that."

That really was his greatest fear. It was understandable. I bet even Spaceman Jack would be afraid of a zombie werewolf.

"Well, do you want a **code word** or something, just in case?" I asked, trying one last time. Ralph might be my enemy, but you know the phrase "I wouldn't wish it on my worst enemy?" I wouldn't wish facing a zombie werewolf on someone alone in the dark—even Ralph.

"How about . . . Scaredy-Cat Sam Wu-ser?" said Ralph with a sneer.

"That's way too long." And just when I was starting to think Ralph and I were on the same team. It looked as if we were back to being enemies. "And by the time you said all that, it would be **WAY** too late."

And then I left him on his own. With his dumb phone.

I stopped by Zoe and Regina's tent, too. The castle tent was **just** as cool as the spaceship tent! They were both already in their sleeping bags and yawning.

"We're all good, Captain Sam," said Zoe.

"We'll see you in the morning," added Regina.

"Mmm, I wonder what we'll have for breakfast?" said Zoe with a yawn. "I'm already hungry."

"Aren't you . . . worried about everything? Like the alien? And whatever is out in the dark?" I asked.

Zoe and Regina looked at each other and shrugged. "My parents are super close," said Regina. "I don't think we have anything to worry about tonight."

"And I'm **SO** tired," said Zoe. "I'm just ready for bed."

"Okay," I said dubiously. There was still **LOTS** to worry about if you asked me. But there was nothing we could do right then about whatever was out in the dark, and I didn't want to freak them out. All part of being a good captain. "Well, goodnight then."

"**Night!**" they said together.

By the time I got back in my tent with Stanley and Bernard, the fire was almost completely out.

It was getting really dark.

Really, **really** dark.

Darker than no man's land dark.

"Should we turn on our flashlights?" I said to Bernard and Stanley.

"What for?" said Stanley with a yawn. "We're going to bed."

"Yeah, and there's nothing to see in here anyway," said Bernard. "I know what we all look like."

"And we don't want the flashlights to run out of battery," added Stanley.

"It was just an idea," I mumbled. Had

132

everyone forgotten about the aliens?

And whatever was hiding in the dark? I wanted to say something, but just like with the girls, I didn't want to worry everyone if there was **nothing** we could do.

I lay in the dark, staring up at the roof of the tent.

At least I thought I was staring at the roof of the tent. It was so dark, I had no idea what I was staring at. I couldn't even see my own hand in front of my face! My eyes might as well have been closed.

I suddenly remembered that Lucy had snuck a night-light in my backpack. I slowly sat up and reached over for my bag.

"Ow!" said Bernard. "What are you doing?"

Whoops. I must have elbowed him.

"Nothing," I said. "I just need to get something from my backpack. Where's the flashlight?"

"I don't know—I can't see where I put it," said Bernard.

"WHAT IS THE POINT OF AN EMERGENCY FLASHLIGHT IF YOU CAN'T FIND IT IN THE DARK?" I exclaimed.

"Calm down, Sam," said Stanley, turning on his flashlight. "What do you need from your backpack?"

I swallowed. What kind of captain would I be if I admitted I wanted a night-light?

"None of your business," I said.

"It's my business if you are rustling around making all that **noise**," grumbled Stanley.

"Just give me my bag, please."

Stanley passed me my backpack. I unzipped it and dug around. There was the night-light! Lucy to the rescue. I'd get it out and wait for the others to go to sleep and then plug it in.

But then, as I gripped it in my hands, I realized something.

There wasn't **anywhere** to plug the night light in.

Of course there wasn't. We were camping. In a tent.

I still owed Lucy one. It wasn't her fault there weren't **any** light sockets out in the woods.

"Lights out, you guys," Bernard's dad called from outside our tent. "I can see a flashlight on. It's time for bed."

Stanley switched it off. And then it was dark again.

✶ ✶ ✶

I lay in my sleeping bag and tried to sleep. First, I lay on my back. Then I switched to my side. Then the other side. Then my stomach. Nothing was working. My brain was **wide awake** as I thought about all the things that could be right outside the tent in the dark.

I made a list in my head. Captain Jane says that when you don't know what to do in a situation, the best thing to do is make a list to know what you're dealing with. Outside in the dark there might be:

* Aliens
* Werewolves
* Zombie werewolves
* Bears
* Bats
* Vampire bats
* Normal wolves
* Monsters
* Ghosts
* The Ghost King
* Snakes (not Fang)
* Any combination of the above
* Other even scarier things I've never even heard of

This was the first time that Captain Jane's advice had **NOT** helped. Making the list just made me realize how many things could be hiding in the dark, and that there was NO way to prepare for all of them. Even a spaceman can only be so brave!

Finally, after about a million hours, I was almost asleep. Then, just as my eyes were closing (at least I think they were—it was so dark that I couldn't tell), something poked me in the side.

"Sam! Sam! Are you awake?" It was Stanley.

"Mmmph," I said into my sleeping bag.

"Sam! Wake up!" He poked me again harder. And then he **PINCHED** me.

"Ow, Stanley! I don't care about your 'jet lag.' Go to sleep!" I said in a loud whisper.

"No, it's not that! Sam, do you hear that?" Stanley whispered back.

"Hear what?"

"Listen!"

"Right now, all I hear is you whispering in my ear."

"Okay, well listen now."

So I did.

Outside the tent, the wind was rustling in the trees, and there were all kinds of eerie creaks and cracks and small squeaks.

CRACK

SQUEAK

CREA

SQUEA

I had been so worried about not being able to see in the dark, I'd **completely forgotten** about listening for danger. I should have known better. After all, I was the one who'd said earlier that we needed

138

to use all of our senses (except taste). When I heard a loud **HOOT**, I sat bolt upright.

"Not *that*—that's just an owl," said Stanley next to me.

"I know that," I whispered back grumpily.

"Keep listening," said Stanley.

There were even more sounds. I listened as hard as I could. I thought I could even hear the gurgling of the stream that I'd fallen into earlier.

There was another crack.

And another.

This one was louder.

And closer.

"**THAT!** Something's out there," whispered Stanley urgently. "We should wake up Bernard."

"I'm already awake," whispered Bernard.

"You guys are so loud."

"Do you hear that noise?" I asked.

"Now I *do*," he whispered back. "What should we do?"

"Nothing," Stanley and I said at the same time.

Suddenly, there was a flash of light right outside our tent.

"Wha-wha-what's that?" stammered Bernard.

"**BE QUIET,**" I whispered back. "We don't want it to know we are in here!"

The light outside moved. Now we could see shadows shifting outside.

"Maybe it's my dad," whispered Bernard.

But then we saw it.

A shape right outside our tent.

And it wasn't Bernard's dad.

It was BIG. Even bigger than his dad.

And it was growling.

"It's a **bear!**" whispered Bernard. "It's going to eat us!"

"It's an alien!" said Stanley in a hushed, panicked voice.

"It's an **ALIEN BEAR!**" I said, because this was obviously the most logical conclusion.

"We have to get my dad!" whispered Bernard, starting to sit up.

I grabbed his arm. "No! We can't go outside! This is the safest place to be. It doesn't know we're here yet.'"

"Then why is it so close?"

There were more cracks and footsteps outside the tent. The big shape was sniffing around our tent. We could hear it breathing.

We all stayed silent.

"**PLAY DEAD,**" I whispered as loudly as I dared. "That's the best thing to do, right?"

"Right," said Stanley.

"How *do* I do that?" whispered Bernard, lying back down again.

"Just close your eyes and lie still," I said.

"I was doing that before you woke me up!"

"Well, do it again!"

"If we're all playing dead, we shouldn't be talking," whispered Stanley.

I heard a twig snap, and I was sure it was right next to our tent. Then there was another **growl**, and this time it was even closer. We all froze.

"Playing dead, playing dead," Bernard mumbled under his breath.

"Play dead quieter," I said.

And then I closed my eyes tight, stayed very still, and hoped that my plan would work.

CHAPTER 14

WHAT'S THE PLAN, CAPTAIN?

I SURVIVED!

It had been a long night. It was hard to play dead when I was sure that **EVERY** noise was something coming to eat me. But I must have fallen asleep at some point because I woke up to the sun shining and birds chirping and Stanley snoring and I'd never been so happy. I thought for sure that whatever was outside our tent last night was going to get us.

I shook Stanley and Bernard awake.

"We made it through the night! Playing dead worked!"

We all **high-fived** our success.

"We should go check on the others," I said. In the daylight, I wasn't afraid of anything.

I bounded out of our tent to see if the others were okay, like a good captain. I was so focused that I nearly stepped in the firepit.

"Whoa, careful there, Sam," said Bernard's dad, pulling me back by the arm. "Those logs are pretty hot. I'm starting up the fire again to make breakfast."

"Mr. Wilson! Did you hear the **monster** last night?" I wasn't sure what exactly we'd heard, but "monster" seemed a pretty good general description that covered most bases.

Bernard's dad yawned. "Can't say that I did. I was out like a log. Ask Bernard—I can sleep through pretty much anything. Now, one time out on a dig . . ."

"Sorry, Mr. Wilson—I've got to go and wake up the others!" I said, running off before he launched into what was sure to be an incredibly long and **boring story** about digging up old stuff.

I tried to knock on Zoe and Regina's castle tent, but because it was fabric, it didn't work very well. So I used my voice instead.

"KNOCK KNOCK! DING DONG! TIME TO WAKE UP!"

I yelled.

Zoe stuck her head outside the tent and yawned. "What *do* you want?"

"You're alive!" I said. "Did Regina make it?"

Regina's head popped out, too. "I did . . . but we heard noises **all night!**" Her eyes were wide.

"I did, too," I said grimly. "Let me go wake up Ralph and then we can compare stories."

I grabbed a pot and metal spoon from beside the fire and went up to Ralph's tent. I banged the pot as loudly as I could to wake him up.

"**WHAT?**" he shouted from inside his tent.

"Just making sure you survived the night!" I yelled.

"Of course I did," said Ralph, coming out of his tent. But he had big circles under his eyes and didn't look like he'd slept at all.

"Are you okay?" I asked. He looked terrible.

"I didn't sleep very much," he admitted.

I lowered my voice. "Did you hear it, too?"

"The growling?" he said.

I nodded. "Yep. What did you do?"

"**Played dead**, of course," he said with a scoff.

"Nicely done," I said, offering my hand in a high-five.

Ralph ignored it.

"I'm going back to bed," he said.

"But we have to stick together today!" I said. "And make the **most** of the daylight. This is when we can search for clues."

Ralph rolled his eyes. "Fine," he said. "But only if we have breakfast first."

✶ ✶✶

Over a campfire breakfast of scrambled eggs, cooked over an open flame, we compared stories.

"I heard the growling, too!" said Regina.

"What about the twigs breaking?"

"And the whistle?"

"I didn't hear a whistle."

"It was right next to my tent!"

"And the footsteps!"

We tried to tell the adults, but they just laughed again.

"We sleep with earplugs, even at home," said Ralph and Regina's mom. "But it sounds as if you heard lots of exciting nature sounds! Owls, perhaps. How very lovely."

"It was more than an owl. There was something **BIG** and **GROWLY** in our campsite," I said. "We all heard it."

"Well, you survived to tell the tale, so that's something," said Bernard's dad.

We all sighed. Even Ralph. There was no way the adults were going to believe us.

✦ ✦✦

"So, what's the plan, Captain?" asked Bernard after we'd finished eating. We had regrouped next to our tents.

I picked up a stick and drew a circle in the dirt. "This is our campsite," I said. I put five triangles inside the circle. "And these are all our tents. We know that the creature in the dark went here, here, and here," I drew its suspected path. "Today our goal is to scout the area for **clues**. Try to figure out where it came from, what it is, and how we can defend ourselves against it if it comes back."

"Sounds like a big job," said Stanley.

I nodded. "It is. Which is why we need to work together. I need **everyone** on this crew to work as a team. Are you with me?" I put my hand out in the middle. Bernard and Zoe stuck their hands in, too. After a second, so did Stanley and Regina.

We all looked at Ralph.

"What *do* you say, Commander?"

He rolled his eyes and flung his own hand

in. "Fine," he said. "But only because I know you

losers will bug me if I don't."

FOR THE UNIVERSE!

"Ralph, if you are going to do this with us, you have to be properly in it," said Regina. "That's the rule."

"Fine," he said, and mumbled something under his breath.

"What was that?" I asked.

"I SAID FOR THE STUPID UNIVERSE," he said.

"For the universe!" we all shouted and shot our hands up in the air.

There we were, a real crew about to start a real adventure.

FOR THE STUPID UNIVERSE!

CHAPTER 15

WHAT LIVES IN CAVES?

Before we could go off on our own adventure, the adults made us hike to a nearby waterfall.

It **was** impressive, for a waterfall, but we didn't find any clues.

Finally, we were allowed to go exploring on our own.

"Stay together and don't go too far," Regina's mom shouted after us.

"And remember, **stay on the path!**" boomed Bernard's dad. He was so loud, I was surprised there wasn't a **rock slide** or an **avalanche**.

As the captain, I led the way.

Until everyone realized I was leading us in circles.

"Sam, this isn't very fun," said Zoe.

"Yeah, you've made us look at the same tree like five times," said Stanley.

"I thought we were going on an adventure," added Regina.

"I knew this would be lame," said Ralph with a smirk.

I couldn't even deny it. I didn't know the first thing about how to track our **mysterious** nighttime visitor.

"It's okay, Captain," said Bernard. "But maybe

155

we should try a

different route next."

"What's down that way?" asked

Stanley, pointing to a small trail off

the main one.

Bernard held up a map. "It's a cave," he said.

"Ohhhh!" said everyone else but me.

A cave sounded **EXACTLY** like the kind of

place a scary nighttime creature would hide

during the day. And the last thing we wanted

to do was to wake it up. I might have felt

braver by daylight, but as far as I knew, caves

were **VERY** dark.

I grabbed the map. "Great research, Chief

Research Officer Bernard," I said. "Now we know

which area to avoid."

Stanley grabbed the map back. "What? No!

I want to see the cave."

"Yeah, me, too," said Ralph. "What's wrong, Sam? Are you **scared?**"

"Of course not," I said. "I just don't want to lead us the wrong way. Or into danger."

"You've already led us in circles," said Ralph with a snort. "We've been following you all day. I think we should go with your cousin Stanley."

I looked around at the rest of my crew. "Is that what you all think?"

No one would look at me.

"We *have* just been going in circles," said Regina quietly.

"But you've done an excellent job of keeping us out of danger," piped Bernard.

At least I can always count on Bernard to be loyal.

＊ ＊＊

As Stanley led us deeper into the woods,
Bernard whispered to me, "What do you think
happens when we get to the cave?"

"What do you mean?" I asked.

"Are we going to go in it?"

"No way!" I said. "Who would want to go
INSIDE a dark cave?"

Turned out, everyone but us.

When we got to the cave opening, Stanley
immediately wanted to go in it.

"But . . . we don't know what's in there!"
I protested.

"What's wrong, Sam?" said Ralph. "Are you
scared?" He snort-laughed.

"I am <u>**NOT**</u> scared," I said hotly. "I'm just
being responsible. What kind of captain would I

be if I sent my crew into uncharted territories?"

"I think you're scared," Ralph scoffed.

"How can *I* be in charge of exploring if we never do any actual exploring?" Zoe interjected. "Isn't the point of exploring to go into uncharted territories? New galaxies? Or caves?"

"Hmmm," I said. I was fighting an uphill battle. Everyone had already made up their minds.

"I've been inside **LOTS** of caves in Hong Kong," said Stanley. "Just make sure you have your flashlight. And watch your head, and where you step. Come on!"

And without waiting for a response from anyone, he went straight in the mouth of the cave.

"Wait for me! I'm coming, too!" said Zoe as she ran after Stanley.

"Me, too!" said Regina.

"Looks like only the losers are staying here," said Ralph as he followed everyone else.

"**This is a very bad idea**," said Bernard, shaking his head. "I've read about caves, and they are **VERY** dangerous and **VERY** dark. And usually filled with bears. Or bats!"

"I don't think we have a choice," I said. "Come on, let's go in. We have to stay with the crew."

It was dark inside the cave.

Once my eyes adjusted, I could see that there were pools of water on the floor and rocky spikes coming from the ceiling. At the end of the cave, it looked as if there were narrow tunnels. Probably going to the center of the earth. **Luckily**, nobody seemed interested in the tunnels.

"This is SO cool!" said Zoe.

"Mmm-hmmm," I said. It wasn't that I was *afraid* in the cave[15], I was just **suspicious** of it. Like any good captain would be in a new territory.

Ralph was turning his flashlight off and on and making shapes on the ceiling.

"So!" I said as loudly as I could, trying to get everyone's attention. My voice echoed in the

---

[15] Because I am NOT afraid of caves.

162

cave. "Sooooo . . . ooo . . . ooo!"

And then of course everyone had to do it. I'll admit, it was pretty fun.

Bernard stood near the entrance of the cave. "I don't like this," he said, but nobody listened to him.

"Hey, guys . . ." Regina said, pointing up above her.

"HelLlllloooOoooO!"

shouted Stanley into the abyss of the cave, ignoring Regina. His voice echoed all around us. It sounded very cool.

"Guuuuuuys," Regina said, waving her arms to get our attention.

"HEEELLllllOOOOOoooO!"

I shouted back at Stanley. My voice echoed

EVERYWHERE. It was awesome.

"I THINK WE NEED TO GET OUT OF HERE!" yelled Regina, running toward me.

And then a dark cloud came down from the cave ceiling, squeaking and flapping.

"ARGH!" we all yelled as we ran for the entrance. Bernard was standing frozen, pointing behind us with his mouth wide open.

"BATS!"

CHAPTER 16

ALIEN INTERFERENCE

We ran—but the bats kept coming! I was pretty sure there were at least a bajillion of them.

"I KNEW THIS WAS A BAD IDEA!" cried Bernard as we ran past him. I grabbed his arm.

"COME ON, BERNARD!" I said. **"I THINK THESE ARE VAMPIRE BATS!"**

In the heat of the moment, my captain instincts took over. "Follow me!" I shouted. I led the group through the trees into a clearing we'd passed earlier. Vampires can't stand the sun.

166

We'd be safe there.

When we finally got to the clearing, we all collapsed on the grass.

"Now *that* was an adventure," said Zoe, grinning.

"WE NEARLY GOT EATEN BY VAMPIRE BATS," said Bernard.

"But we didn't!" said Zoe with a fist pump.

"Do you really think those were vampire bats?" said Regina.

"Of course they were," I said. "And now we know what was outside our tent last night. **VAMPIRES**."

I turned to Bernard. "Chief Research Officer, what do we know about vampires?"

"I didn't do any vampire research!" Bernard wailed. "I was expecting bears! Or wolves!"

"I know!" said Stanley. "We can use Ralph's phone."

Ralph frowned. "Do we have to?"

"That's an **order**, Commander," I said as sternly as I could.

"And I'll tell Mom and Dad that you wouldn't share," added Regina.

"Fine," muttered Ralph, reaching into his pocket. Then he gasped. "It won't turn on!"

We all crowded around him.

"Let me see," said Stanley, reaching for the phone. "Ralph's right—it's dead."

"There's only one explanation," I said grimly.

Everyone looked at me.

"**Alien interference**."

"Aliens?" gasped Regina.

I nodded. I was sure of it. "We're not just

168

dealing with vampires here. Oh no. This is something much, much bigger," I said.

"Bigger than what?" asked Stanley.

I frowned. "Just **bigger**," I said, stretching out my arms for emphasis.

"So what are we going to do?" asked Bernard.

"Go back to base! I'll tell you there."

"Base?" said Regina.

"He means our campsite," said Zoe. "You'll understand SPACE BLASTERS speak soon, don't worry."

* **

We didn't tell the grown-ups about the bats because we knew we'd get into trouble for going off the main path.

"So, what's the plan, Sam?" said Stanley.

"Here's what we're going to do," I said.

I picked up a stick and started drawing in the dirt again.

"This," I said, putting a rock in the center of a circle, "is the fire. As long as we keep the fire going all night, I think we should be safe from vampires."

"But how will we do that?" said Regina.

"We'll take shifts and stay up all night. It's the only way. And we'll do it in pairs. Safety in numbers."

"What about the aliens?" asked Zoe. "Will the fire keep them away?"

I wasn't sure. But a captain can never show uncertainty.

"Yes," I said confidently. "Aliens hate fire. And water! So we'll keep a bucket of water next to the fire, too. If anyone sees an alien, they should throw water on it."

"But, Sam, what if the alien's from a water planet?" said Bernard.

"Then the fire will keep them away! It's a foolproof plan," I said. I didn't mention the other types of aliens that loved fire **AND** water, but I just had to hope we weren't dealing with those.

"Won't Bernard's dad try to put the fire out before bed, like he did last night?" asked Stanley.

"This is where the plan gets tricky," I said.

"*This* is where the plan gets tricky?" scoffed Ralph. "This whole thing sounds **RIDICULOUS!**"

"Listen to Captain Sam, Ralph," said Regina. "He knows what he's doing."

"He *does* not," said Ralph, but Regina frowned at him. "Okay, okay," Ralph relented. "What *do* we do then?"

"Okay. So tonight, after Bernard's dad has put the fire out and gone to bed, one of us will have to start the fire back up again," I said.

"Who knows how to do that?" asked Zoe.

I looked at Stanley, who smiled at me and gave me a **thumbs up**.

"Our camping expert. Colonel Stanley," I said proudly.

Who knew Stanley's camping expertise would **actually** come in handy?

✦ ✦✦

We agreed on our shifts. Stanley and Ralph first, then Regina and Zoe, and Bernard and I would take the last watch.

"What's the code word if we see anything suspicious?" asked Stanley.

"Scaredy-Cat Sam Wu-s—"

"Ralph!" Regina jumped in.

"Hoot like an owl **three times**," I said, ignoring Ralph and giving Regina a smile.

We all practiced hooting.

"And what do we do if we hear a hoot?" asked Zoe.

"We all run out of our tents and help our crew members," I said.

HOOT HOOT HOOT HOHOOT HOOT HOOT

"This is the bravest thing we've **EVER** done," said Zoe.

"I've never done anything like this before," agreed Regina. "It's exciting!"

"It's stupid," said Ralph, rolling his eyes.

I turned to Ralph. "Commander, this is serious business. Are you in or are you out?"

"Why does everyone keep asking me that? I'm in, I'm in, okay? **Jeez**."

"Good."

"But only so the aliens don't get us," Ralph added.

"Or the zombie werewolf," said Regina.

"I still think it might have been a bear," said Bernard with a shudder.

"Whatever it is that comes out in the dark, we'll be ready," I said.

＊ ＊＊

Everything started perfectly.

After Bernard's dad went to bed and we could hear him snoring, Stanley crept out of the tent and started up the fire again.

"Don't forget to wake up Zoe and Regina," I said. I was **so excited** and awake I kind of wished I was taking the first watch, but I knew it made sense for it to be Stanley and Ralph. Mostly because Bernard and I didn't know how to start a fire.

I must have fallen asleep at some point, because suddenly Zoe was shaking me awake.

"It's your turn," she said with a yawn. "None of us have seen anything **suspicious**."

I rubbed my eyes and poked Bernard.

We sat out by the fire which was smaller now.

"It's cold out here," said Bernard, shivering.

I nodded. It was. And I was sleepy. I could hear Bernard's dad snoring loudly in his tent.

"I'm going to get my sleeping bag," Bernard said.

"Good idea," I said. "Can you get mine, too? And leave the tent unzipped in case we need to get back in really fast."

Bernard came out of our tent, his arms full of sleeping bags. "Stanley looked like he was having a **weird dream**. He was flailing around and stuff."

"Yeah, he does that sometimes," I said. "It keeps me awake when we're sharing a room."

Bernard nodded.

I wiggled into my sleeping bag while Bernard did the same. "Hey, why don't we sit back-to-back?" I suggested. "That way nothing can sneak up behind us."

We sat like that for a while, listening as hard as we could for **anything**.

"Hey, Sam," said Bernard.

"Mmm-hmmm?"

"What do you think it really was? The thing we heard last night?"

"It could have been anything," I said. "You

never know in the dark."

"Makes sense," said Bernard.

I watched the fire. I knew I should have been more **scared**, but I was so sleepy.

"Hey, Sam," Bernard said again.

"Yeah, Bernard?" I said with a yawn.

"Keeping watch is pretty boring, isn't it?"

"Mmm-hmmm," I said.

He was right. And I was so tired…

And before I knew it, my head was tilting forward and my eyes were closing . . .

✳ ✳ ✳

"OH NO! THE FIRE'S OUT!"

How long had I been asleep for?

"Bernard!" I said, elbowing him. "Bernard, wake up!"

Bernard jolted awake. "What? What? Where am I?"

"We fell asleep! The fire is out!
And it's **DARK!**"

I couldn't see **ANYTHING**.

"Oh no!" said Bernard.

"Quick! Get back in the tent!" We jumped
out of our sleeping bags and rushed back
into the tent.

"Phew! That was a close one," said Bernard.

"We've **messed everything up!** We let the fire out! How will we stay safe from the vampires and the bears and the aliens now?" I moaned.

"Let's just wake up Stanley—he'll be able to start the fire again," said Bernard.

"Bernard, you're a genius!" I said.

"I know," said Bernard. "But, Sam?"

"Yeah?"

"Where's Stanley?"

CHAPTER 17

HOOT-HOOT-HOOT!

"What do you mean, *where's Stanley?*" I said.

"He's not here!" Bernard said.

I felt around blindly in the tent.

Bernard was right.

Stanley was gone.

Bernard ran outside the tent and started hooting.

"Just three hoots!" I said. He'd done about ten. "Otherwise they won't know it's the code word!"

HOOT HOOT HOOT HOOT HOOT HOOT HOOT

"Sorry!" he said.

We did three loud hoots together.

"Now what?" said Bernard.

I hadn't thought this through. "They should be coming," I said. "Or at least hooting back."

"Maybe we should try again?"

"Hoot-hoot-hoot!"

Still nothing.

"Sam," said Bernard. "You know I love a code word, but maybe we should just wake them up?"

"Good idea," I said. "You get Zoe and Regina. I'll get Ralph."

"Should we get my dad?"

I paused. I knew that if we woke up Bernard's dad, I would have failed as a captain.

"Not yet," I said. "I think this is something the crew can handle."

I went into Ralph's tent and poked him.

"What is it?" he said.

"Stanley's been taken," I said. Because at this point, it was the only possibility.

"**WHAT?**" said Ralph, sitting straight up.

"Come on," I said. "We've got to find him."

"Go out in the woods in the dark? No way!"

"We have to!"

"I'm waking up my parents," Ralph said.

"**SAM, COME HERE RIGHT NOW!**" yelled Bernard.

"Come on," I said, yanking Ralph's arm. "There's no time to wake up your parents!"

"**SAM!**" shouted Bernard.

"That'll wake them up anyway," said Ralph.

We stumbled out of the tent and I saw why Bernard was yelling for us.

183

Coming right at us from the dark woods was a strange figure, walking with its arms stretched straight out!

"IT'S A ZOMBIE!" yelled Ralph.

"IT'S AN ALIEN!" yelled Bernard.

"IT'S A VAMPIRE!" yelled Regina.

"IT'S STANLEY!" I cried. I recognized his pajamas.

"STANLEY'S BEEN TURNED INTO A VAMPIRE! HE MUST HAVE BEEN BITTEN BY A BAT!" shouted Bernard.

Oh no. That hadn't even occurred to me.

"EVERYONE STOP YELLING!" yelled Zoe.

Then, more quietly, she added, "Sam, you have to try to talk to him. He's your cousin."

"Yeah," agreed Bernard.

"And maybe he won't bite you."

I took a deep breath. They were right.

It was up to me.

I held my flashlight out in front of me and walked toward Vampire Stanley.

"Stanley," I said when I was closer. "It's me, Sam. Wu Gabo! Your cousin!"

He kept walking toward me with his arms stretched out.

"Stanley! Stop! It's me! We're family!

DON'T BITE ME!"

He kept coming.

Oh no. I definitely didn't want to turn into a vampire, too.

He was so close now. This was it. I either had to turn and run or be bitten by a vampire.

Wait. Was he . . . snoring?

"STANLEY!" I yelled as loud as I could and clapped my hands in his face.

He opened his eyes.

"Sam?" he said. "What are we doing? Why are we outside?"

"What are YOU doing?" I asked.

He looked down at his feet. They were covered in mud. "Uh-oh, was I sleep walking? I do that sometimes. Sorry. I probably should have mentioned it."

"WHAT'S HAPPENING OVER THERE?" shouted Zoe.

186

"DO YOU NEED BACKUP?"

I was so relieved that we'd found Stanley, and that he wasn't a vampire, that I just started laughing.

"He's fine!" I yelled back to Zoe and the rest of the crew.

Stanley and I walked back to everyone and we high-fived and cheered for **saving the day**. Or, I guess technically, we'd saved the night.

I still couldn't believe that the grown-ups were sleeping through all of this.

Then Bernard started hooting. "Hoot-hoot-hoot!" he said, his eyes wide as he pointed behind me.

"Bernard, we're all here. We don't need the code word any more," I said.

187

"LOOK BEHIND YOU, SAM!"

he shouted.

I heard a loud growl. Just like the one I'd heard the night before.

I turned.

THERE WAS A HUGE HAIRY CREATURE COMING TOWARD US!

I yelled the only captain command possible in this situation.

"RUN!"

CHAPTER 18

THE CREATURE IN THE DARK

We all ran in different directions in the camp.

"IT'S THE ZOMBIE WEREWOLF!" cried Ralph. "I DON'T WANT IT TO EAT ME! MOM!"

"HE'S RIGHT!" yelled Regina, as they ran toward their parents' tent.

"IT'S A BEAR!" shouted Bernard. "DAAAAAD!"

I was sure it was an alien. Some kind of big, furry alien with glowing yellow eyes.

A very small part of me wanted to run away on my own and leave the others to deal with the **alien monster**. But that isn't what a captain does. So I summoned all of my bravery.

"General Zoe! Grab me that bucket of water!" I yelled. It was our last hope.

Zoe grabbed it and raced over to me. I could see the furry alien coming even closer. It was snarling. And it looked as if it was multiplying! There was another **HUGE** shadow behind it! This was it. I pulled my arm back and flung the water over the creature.

RIGHT AS THE ALIEN CREATURE JUMPED ON ME AND STARTED TO EAT MY FACE!

Wait.

It was just licking my face.

"Down, girl," said the voice. "You're bigger than this kid. Don't want to give him a heart attack."

The creature dropped down and barked.

A DOG? It must have been an alien dog. Although now that someone was shining a flashlight on it, it did look a lot like a normal dog. Just a **HUGE** one. A huge, wet dog.

"What is going on?" said Bernard's dad, coming out of his tent with Bernard. "Oh hi, Ben! Nice to see you, even in the middle of the night."

"MR. WILSON, YOU'RE WORKING

WITH THE ALIEN?" I shouted. I thought he was on our side!

Bernard's dad yawned. "Sam, I don't know what you are talking about, but this is my good friend, Ranger Ben. He works here in the woods as a mountain ranger. We're going to have lunch with him tomorrow in his cabin."

I looked up at the alien man. There were enough flashlights on now that I could get a good look at him.

He was even bigger than Bernard's dad!

And he had a **HUGE** beard and long hair and if he wasn't an alien, I was sure he was a wild mountain man. Definitely half-bear.

"What is going on out here?" said Regina's mom, coming out of her tent in a dressing gown. "Ralph and Regina are talking **gibberish**." She spotted Ranger Ben. "Oh, hello there."

"I'm very confused," said Stanley, sitting down.

"Look, Ralph! It's not a zombie werewolf! It's just a giant man. And a giant dog!" said Regina.

Zoe went up to pet the dog. "What kind of dog is this, sir?"

"Oh, Rocky is a bit of a mix. Not quite sure. I bet she's part **wolf** though."

I took a step back, but Zoe kept on petting the wolf dog.

194

"Now, what I want to know," said Ranger
    Ben, "is why you are all awake in the middle
    of the night and why you threw **water** at me
and my dog?"

Bernard's dad raised his eyebrows. "Sounds
like Sam and Bernard all right."

"We thought you were an alien," I said.

"Or maybe a bear," added Bernard.

"Or a vampire," said Regina.

"Or some kind of monster that lives in the
dark," said Stanley.

"I see," said Ranger Ben, stroking his beard.
"Sorry to disappoint you all. It's just me and
Rocky. At night, we patrol to make sure the
fires are out and that **everything is okay**."

"Wait!" said Zoe. "Did you come by our camp
last night?"

195

"Sure did," said Ranger Ben.

It all made sense now! The sniffing! The footsteps! It was Ranger Ben and Rocky!

"Sounds like you've all had quite the **adventure**," said Ranger Ben. "I heard a bit of commotion, so I came by to check on you guys." He looked up at the other grown-ups. "How did you sleep through all that racket?"

"Earplugs," said Ralph and Regina's mom.

"Heavy sleeper," said Bernard's dad.

"Well, I was about to go check out the **meteor shower**. Since you're all awake now, do you want to come with me?"

"The meteor shower?" I asked. "What meteor shower?"

"Just the biggest one in over a hundred years! And it's happening right above us.

It's been all over the news—haven't you heard about it?" said Ranger Ben.

Something occurred to me.

"Ralph! That must have been what we were seeing on your phone!" I turned to Ranger Ben. "We thought they were UFOs," I explained. "That's why we thought you were an alien."

"A completely understandable mistake," said Ranger Ben with a laugh. "I'm a bit of a **space fan** myself."

I looked up, hoping to spot a meteor, but I could only see the dark branches of the trees and an occasional glimpse of black sky. "I can't see anything," I said.

"The trees are blocking our view here," said Ranger Ben. "Follow me and bring your flashlights for the walk."

CHAPTER 19

SPACE BLASTERS IN THE SKY

Some people[16] might think that walking through a dark forest at night would be scary, but I wasn't afraid at all! Probably because I was walking next to Ranger Ben. And having a wolf dog on your side also helps. We were pretty much **invincible**.

We followed Ranger Ben to a clearing.

"All right, everyone, come and sit down here. Now, I need you all to turn off your flashlights."

---

[16] Definitely not me, because I'm never afraid.

"What?" I said. "But then it will be **TOTALLY** dark!" Even after everything that had happened tonight, I didn't want to turn off my flashlight.

"Just trust me," said Ranger Ben. "Some things are best in the dark."

So we all turned off our flashlights and looked up into the night sky.

And then the most **AMAZING** thing happened! It was like fireworks, but **BETTER!** There were shooting stars everywhere!

"Whoa!" said Ralph.

"Wow!" said Zoe.

"This is **AWESOME!**" said Stanley. "I've never seen a meteor shower before. Not even in Hong Kong!"

"So cool!" said Bernard.

I couldn't say anything. It was the closest I'd

ever felt to being a real spaceman. All I could do was stare at the sky above me and watch the meteor shower.

And at one point, I was sure I saw **TUBS**[17] carrying the **SPACE BLASTERS** crew across the universe. I waved, just in case Captain Jane and Spaceman Jack could see me down on earth.

---

[17] The Universe's Best Spaceship.

CHAPTER 20

MASTERS OF THE DARK

The next morning, it was time to pack up camp.

I never thought I'd say this, but I didn't want to leave.

The night before seemed like a dream, but I knew it was real. Partly because Ranger Ben and Rocky the wolf dog were there helping us take down our tents.

"We did it again, Sam," said Bernard as we rolled up our sleeping bags. "We prepared for the unpreparable, and we **survived**."

This is to certify SAM WU is officially a Master of the Dark

"We're going to need certificates for this," said Zoe. "I'm thinking '**Masters of the Dark**.'"

"I like it," I said.

"Do I get one?" asked Regina.

"Of course!" said Zoe.

"I don't want a stupid certificate," said Ralph, turning up his nose. "I'm ready to go home to my own bed and my real friends."

I stuck my hand out. "Well, it was a pleasure having you on my crew, Commander Ralph."

He looked at my hand for a long time.

And then he shook it. "I guess it wasn't **too terrible** . . . Captain Sam."

I beamed.

"But I still don't think you're brave enough to take on the zombie werewolf in our basement," he added.

I looked at the rest of my crew. "I think we can take it on," I said. "I think our crew can take on anything."

Because I'm Sam Wu, and I am **<u>NOT</u>** afraid.

Katie and Kevin are definitely __NOT__ afraid of answering some author questions ❗❗

Sam's camping trip was SO much fun! Have you guys ever been camping? And did anything super scary happen?

We love camping! We've camped all over the world, from beaches in Hong Kong to mountains in Peru to the Serengeti in Africa! One night camping in Africa we heard lions roaring, which was pretty scary! We stayed inside our tent.

If you could pack 5 MUST HAVE things in a backpack like Sam's, what would you pack? (Ours might be something beginning with "marsh" and ending in "mallows")

1. Definitely marshmallows!
2. Flashlight
3. Bug spray to keep away mosquitoes!
4. A swimsuit in case we find a lake or river to swim in
5. A water bottle to stay hydrated

Were you ever afraid of the dark?

Kevin: I was only scared of my basement in the dark, other than that the dark never bothered me.

Katie: I always kept the hall light on at night, just in case I had to leave my room to go to the bathroom.

Sam tells Bernard that "books won't save you from bears" but have any books saved YOU from being afraid of anything?

Katie: I loved a book called *Julie of the Wolves* when I was younger, and it taught me a lot about wolves and made me curious about them instead of afraid.

Kevin: I read a lot of books about sharks . . . but I'm still pretty afraid of them!

When you go camping, there are LOTS of creepy spiders! Is there anything you might want to mention about our eight-legged friends . . . ?

Sam might not face any spiders while camping, but he'll have to face them in the next book . . . *Sam Wu is Not Afraid of Spiders!* You'll have to read the book to find out where he comes face to face with a **giant spider!**

ACKNOWLEDGMENTS

We love writing Sam Wu—but we couldn't have made it into a real book that you can hold in your hands without the help and support of some amazing people!

If we had our own spaceship on *Space Blasters*, our captain would be Claire Wilson, our fearless agent who always guides us in the right direction. Thank you for believing in us and believing in Sam Wu.

We are tremendously grateful to everyone at both our U.S. and U.K. publishers, Sterling Publishing and Egmont, for supporting Sam Wu. Special thank you to our brilliant editors, Rachael Stein at Sterling and Lindsey Heaven at Egmont, for all their hard work on the book. We've loved working with you! Thank you as well to our copyeditors, Brian Phair at Sterling and Catherine Coe at Egmont.

A huge thank you to our incredibly talented illustrator Nathan Reed for bringing Sam and his friends to life on the page! The illustrations are our favorite part of the book and they somehow keep getting better and better! We are very lucky authors.

Thank you as well to our wonderful designer, Lizzie Gardiner at Egmont, who made the pages look so awesome. And thank you to the publicity, sales, and marketing teams for supporting the books on both sides of the pond, especially Sari Lampert Murray and Lauren Tambini at Sterling

We'd like to thank our families and friends for all their support and excitement. Special thank you to our grandparents: Mimi, Pop-Pop, Grandpa Bob, and Po-Po. And huge thanks and love to Katie's siblings, Jack and Jane; Kevin's sister, Stephanie; and our brother- and sister-in-law, Ben and Cat. And shout-out to our nephew, Cooper, for being the cutest Space Blaster in the whole universe!

And thank you to our parents, for everything.

Turn the page for a sneak peek at Sam's next exciting adventure!

SAM WU
is NOT afraid of
SPIDERS

Nope, totally NOT worried!!!!!

KATIE & KEVIN TSANG

Illustrated by Nathan Reed

The school tarantula has escaped from her cage, and Sam Wu is the only one brave enough to save everyone. What could *possibly* go wrong?

STERLING CHILDREN'S BOOKS
New York

CHAPTER 1

SPIDERS ARE SNEAKY

My name is **Sam Wu**, and I am <u>**NOT**</u> afraid of spiders.

I recently went on a camping trip. You might think camping out in the woods is where I had to face spiders, but no. That was where I had to prove I was <u>**NOT**</u> afraid of the dark.

It is very dark in the woods. And only the **BRAVEST** can survive

spending the night out in the dark. Luckily, I was with my **best friends** Bernard and Zoe, and we came up with a plan. Less luckily, I was also there with my cousin Stanley, who is kind of a know-it-all, and Ralph, who is my nemesis. We've been enemies for a long time. He was the one who first started calling me **Scaredy-Cat Sam**, which forced me to prove to everyone how brave I was.

Anyway, it was a close call, but we survived the dark. And I know part of the reason was because I kept thinking what **Spaceman Jack**

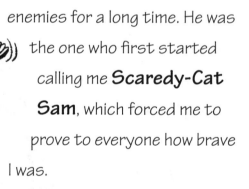

and **Captain Jane** would do![1] Whenever I'm in a tough situation, I imagine them right there with me.

And, before the dark, I had to face sharks *and* ghosts! I'm now

an experienced shark evader, certified ghost-hunter, and on top of all of that, I'm a seasoned snake wrangler. Even **Spaceman Jack** is afraid of snakes!

---

[1] Spaceman Jack and Captain Jane are the main characters on SPACE BLASTERS which is the best show in the whole universe! They have lots of adventures, and I want to be just like them. Ralph says he thinks the show sounds stupid, but he doesn't know what he's talking about.

I thought that after everything that had happened, with surviving the dark, that things would feel different at school, but life continued as normal.

I was still best friends with Zoe and Bernard. My cousin Stanley went back to

Hong Kong, and I actually missed him. Even though he's a know-it-all, he can be kind of useful sometimes.

And Ralph was still my nemesis. I thought maybe he'd be nicer after we survived the dark together and solved the mystery of what had been creeping around our campsite, but I was wrong. He still called me Sam Wu-ser and

made fun of **SPACE BLASTERS**.
We were definitely <u>**NOT**</u>
friends.

Ralph's twin sister,
Regina, who had also been
camping with us, was still
nice. Even nicer in fact.

My little sister, Lucy, was still
the actual bravest person I knew, and her cat

Butterbutt was usually
to blame for most
things.

I thought
that my time of
facing my fears
was behind me.
After all, I'd

already faced ghosts, sharks, and the dark. But then came the **SPIDERS!**

After everything, I thought I'd be prepared. Because here's the thing about spiders. They're sneaky. They can get you when you least expect them. And before you know it— BAM—they have you in their web.

It would be up to me to save everyone. Just like Spaceman Jack would do.

CHAPTER 2

TULIP THE TARANTULA

To be honest, I'd never thought that much about spiders before.

I'd seen them, of course, making webs in the garden or in a corner of the kitchen, but they'd always been small. And I didn't like the feeling of walking into a spiderweb, feeling its sticky strands getting caught on me, almost like getting a hug from a ghost. But, really, it was easy to brush the web away and carry on with my adventures.

My friend Bernard, however, had thought a **LOT** about spiders.

Bernard is the smartest kid in our whole grade, and he loves facts. Every day, he tells us a new fact about something. Some are more interesting than others.

On this day, they were all

about spiders.

"Did you know," he said as he put on his glasses[2], "the silk in a spider's web is five times stronger than a strand of steel? Or that there are almost forty thousand

---

[2] Bernard doesn't actually need glasses, but he likes to put on a pair of "thinking" glasses before he says something smart, which is at least three times a day.

different types of spiders?"

Zoe shuddered and ran her hands through her hair like she was looking for tiny spiders.

"Or did you know that they don't use muscles in their legs, but move using hydraulic pressure? Like **ROBOTS!**"

"I did not know that," I admitted. "Why have you been researching so much about spiders?"

"Don't you remember?" Bernard replied. "Today the sixth graders are coming to our class to show us the tarantula that lives in their science lab."

I frowned. I'd heard of tarantulas, but I couldn't one hundred percent remember what they were.

Bernard sensed my confusion. "Big, hairy spiders," he said, his eyes huge. "I've never seen one in real life, just in pictures."

I swallowed. "No big deal," I said, even though my heart was starting to beat very fast. "I bet Fang could beat a tarantula in a battle. He'd probably eat it for breakfast."

Fang is my **VERY** fierce, **VERY** dangerous pet snake. He's my sidekick, and only the bravest people in the world, like me, can handle him. I got him at the pet store a while back to prove how brave I was.

My little sister, Lucy, thinks she can hold him, but she doesn't understand how ferocious he is, even though I've told her a million times. She thinks he's cute. Which is ridiculous!

"I don't know," Bernard said,

shaking his head. "Fang is pretty ferocious, but I think tarantulas can take down prey over twice their size. And they actually *do* have fangs."

Bernard says Fang is misnamed because he *technically* doesn't have fangs, but I think the name suits him perfectly.

I swallowed again. I didn't like the idea of coming face-to-face with *anything* that had fangs.

"I like spiders," Regina chimed in, pushing her hair out of her eyes. "Do you think they'll let us hold it?"

"Probably not," I said quickly. "Just for everyone's safety." I turned to Bernard. "Right, Bernard?"

He shrugged. "I don't know," he said. "They're sixth graders. Who knows what they'll *do*."

⋆ ⋆⋆

Word spread quickly about the spiders and
the sixth graders coming to our class. Our
teacher, Ms. Winkleworth, had to put four
names on the Not Listening
Board and clap her
hands six times
before we settled
down.

Luckily, my
name wasn't
on the board.
Neither was
Zoe's or Bernard's
or Regina's. Or
Ralph's—but that
wasn't lucky. I wouldn't

have minded seeing his name up there.

"Now, class," said Ms. Winkleworth, "we're going to be on our very best behavior for our sixth grade visitors, correct?"

"Yes, Ms. Winkleworth," we all chorused back.

"And we'll stay in our seats and only talk when we're called on, correct?"

"Yes, Ms. Winkleworth."

"Very good," she said. "I don't want to put anyone else's name on the board."

We all sat in silence. My heart was beating very fast inside my chest, but that was because I was ready for anything. I used to think this feeling meant I was nervous, but now I know it is the feeling I get when I need to be extra brave.

The door opened and
four sixth graders walked
in with their science teacher,
Mr. Dougal.

And he was holding a

HUGE

spider.

In his hands!

Sam Wu is absolutely, positively, definitely <u>NOT</u> afraid!

Discover the first two books in this **LAUGH-OUT-LOUD** series.

STERLING CHILDREN'S BOOKS
New York